my not-so-still Life

my not-so-still Life

liz gallagher

EMBER

Text copyright © 2011 by Liz Gallagher
Cover art copyright © 2011 by Ericka O'Rourke

All rights reserved. Published in the United States by Ember, an imprint of Random House Children's Books, a division of Random House, Inc., New York. Originally published in hardcover in the United States by Wendy Lamb Books, an imprint of Random House Children's Books, New York, in 2011.

Ember and the colophon are trademarks of Random House, Inc.

Visit us on the Web! randomhouse.com/teens

Educators and librarians, for a variety of teaching tools, visit us at randomhouse.com/teachers

The Library of Congress has cataloged the hardcover edition of this work as follows:
Gallagher, Liz.
My not-so-still life / by Liz Gallagher. — 1st ed.
p. cm.
ISBN 978-0-375-84154-5 (trade) — ISBN 978-0-375-94330-0 (lib. bdg.) —
ISBN 978-0-375-89974-4 (ebook) [1. Interpersonal relations—Fiction. 2. Dating (Social customs)—Fiction. 3. Friendship—Fiction. 4. Art—Fiction. 5. High schools—Fiction. 6. Schools—Fiction. 7. Seattle (Wash.)—Fiction.] I. Title.
PZ7.G13556My 2011
[Fic]—dc22
2010038546

ISBN 978-0-375-84155-2 (pbk.)

RL: 6.0

Printed in the United States of America

10 9 8 7 6 5 4 3 2 1

First Ember Edition 2012

Random House Children's Books supports the First Amendment and celebrates the right to read.

To all the friends
who waited for this book,
especially Bruce Wylie,
who lived so beautifully

my not-so-still Life

One

It's time for a new color.

I drape my Smurfette towel over my shoulders and yell, "I'm ready for pink!"

Nick joins me in my bathroom. He unpacks the bleach kit, the bottle of dye.

We do this so often, we've got it down to a science. Nick gets everything prepped, using the back of the toilet as his work space.

An hour later, I'm blowing my new hair dry while Nick plays with eyeliner at my desk.

"The pink looks hot," he says when I come out of the bathroom. "It's so bright."

"I love it," I say. It reminds me of cherry blossoms, my favorite.

Here's why I change my hair color so much: All the talent in the world doesn't equal an actual personality. It's not enough to only make the art. You have to *be* the artist.

Since sixth grade I've been all sorts of other colors. They were all starting to blend on top of each other, though, so it was a mess. Now that we've bleached it out and started over with the pink, I feel like myself, like a good version of me, like something worth looking at, twice. And that's what I want. If people don't notice me, why should I do anything? Why even exist?

"Nice job coloring in the lines," I say to Nick.

"Coloring in the lines" is all about comics. Nick likes to draw, but he's better at doing color than outlines. He and a boy called Jewel started a strip together freshman year, before I was close with either of them. Not that I'm close with Jewel anymore.

Their strip lasted for only a few months. They'd get color copies at the copy shop by school and put a stack on a table during each of their lunch periods, all nonchalant, like they didn't care if anyone picked it up or not. People did. I'm not totally sure why the guys stopped, except that neither one of them seems to have a long attention span. Not for projects, and not for relationships.

In comics, there's the penciler, the inker, and the colorist. Sometimes they're all the same person, and some-

times people are great at one or two parts, so they special-
ize. The penciler sketches the general feeling of each panel.
That was Jewel. The inker does the outlines, the black, the
final artwork. That was Jewel, too. The colorist does the
color, the lighting, the shading. That's Nick, prettying up
everything around him.

That's me, too, in general. A colorist. Giving life to a
black-and-white world.

Nick's pretty colorful himself, at least in his clothes. Jet-
black hair works on him, so he's kept that up since the fall,
and it looks especially good when he wears his neon tank
tops and tees. He loves his eighties hoodie with the
electric-blue star on the back, outlined in silver glitter.

He's actually dialed it down, adding jeans and sneakers
to the mix, but for a while there in the fall, he always
looked like he was on his way to a rave. He's the sweetest
guy you've ever met, though, and he doesn't go to raves.

Tonight, he's wearing my black T-shirt with the metallic stars, his favorite Euro-style jeans, and his silver adidas
Superstars. He dresses the same whether he's at school,
hanging out in my bedroom, or going out, which for us usually means taking the bus to grab coffee or food and watch
Seattle go by while Seattle watches us.

I'm in my black cotton tank dress. It's stained with
paint splotches and drips of bleach from various hair exper-
iments, and those stains are the reason it's my favorite
thing to wear around the house. At school, I dress in a way

my mom considers "wild," but really it's not that crazy. When I go out, I wear school-type clothes with more intense makeup.

"I nuked you a snack," Nick says, nodding toward the plate on my bed. My mom and Grampie always stock our freezer with microwave burritos, the healthy ones with the whole-wheat tortillas. Except for the weeks after they do their big salmon grab.

They love salmon, the ocean, and Puget Sound. Grampie was a lifer longshoreman until he retired last year, and Mom still works at the docks. Grampie jokes that they have water in their veins.

They go out fishing with a friend on his boat, leaving the port in Ballard before sunrise, and they fish salmon till the sun goes down. They do this for a solid week. Then they host this party in our tiny backyard for everyone we know, and they smoke the salmon.

Burritos are more to my liking. I sit down to munch. "Thanks."

Nick's eating at my desk. He went minimal with his eyes, just a touch of brown liner at the outside corners.

He picks up my phone and snaps a photo of me when I'm off guard. "To show Holly your hair," he says. My friend Holly doesn't usually leave her house on weeknights, except for orchestra practice.

"Send it," I say, so Nick does.

Mom pokes her head in the door. Her curly brown hair

is in a messy ponytail as usual, and she has zero makeup on. At least she keeps a decent tan from working outside. It's not the kind of tan you'd get in a sunny place, of course, but the sun does break through, even in Seattle, and she does ten-hour shifts at the docks. She's in her gray sweats. You can tell how strong she is from her hard work. Still, she's feminine. Her voice is so warm. "Pink. Hmmm. Not bad."

"Thanks," I say.

Mom looks at Nick before going back to the family room to watch TV with Grampie. "Ten o'clock, hon."

"Time flies when you're coloring Vanessa." He grabs his backpack and I walk him to the front door, give him a quick hug goodbye. "Art walk tomorrow night?"

"Absolutely," I say. "Holly might be able to come too."

"Superb." He heads out the door.

I've slept in the same bed my whole life, and it was my mom's before it was mine. We still live in the house where she grew up, with my Grampie. I sleep in my mom's childhood bedroom; she sleeps in the master bedroom; Grampie sleeps in the converted basement.

On weekdays, when I wake up, Mom's already at work at the docks. She's up before dawn. Grampie's usually at the kitchen table with the crossword. I'm almost always running late for school.

My dad's never been around. I think of Grampie more

as a dad. My actual dad is Paul, my mom's high school boyfriend. He lives near San Diego now, and has a wife but no other kids. His parents feel so guilty about him getting Mom pregnant, they help out with raising me. Financially, that is. They paid for me to go to Ocean Tides for middle school, and they'd happily have kept paying for me to go to private high school, but I didn't want to. No way was I wearing a uniform. I think what they really feel guilty about is that Paul got to go off to college and build a normal life, while Mom stayed here, stuck to me.

Every day, I wear a string around my wrist—different colors representing how I'm feeling. My string scale follows the spectrum—purple is the best, then blue, green, yellow, orange, red, and then black. Last fall, when my heart got mashed, I wore black.

I started the strings during middle school at Ocean Tides, in the art room on a day that must've been one of the first times I ever really thought about personal expression. The art room had this green shag rug in one corner, and we'd sit there to have "verbal exploration," as our art teacher, Bobby, called it. That day, we were talking about the color wheel and how colors can bounce off each other. He wanted us to do a self-portrait with a focus on color. I froze. I just could not decide what color best represented me. I haven't really stopped thinking about it since.

Today, I go for a blue string.

After I pick out the string every day, I pick out an outfit, usually a skirt that my mom will say is too short, and a top that's either black or super-bright. Today: denim and black.

I pile on jewelry. I've made most of it myself. Lots of paper-clip bracelets and pop-top necklaces. Grampie lets me use his drill when I want to make beads out of found objects like the pop-tops, a guitar pick from a show at Vera Project, a little star I whittled in Mr. Smith's art workshop at school.

I consider where I would get a tattoo. Correction: where I *will* get a tattoo. Some days, I want one on my ankle. Or the inside of my forearm. I think about my lower back and my rib cage. I want to cover my whole body with ink and become a piece of art.

Mom says no, that I'm too young to know what I want. I've agreed to wait till I'm eighteen. Two more years. Not that I expect much to change by then.

I do my makeup. Usually some purple on my eyes, and lots of liner and mascara. My lips explore a range from shimmery nude to black. When Nick does my makeup, he might choose pinks, but I almost never do. Sometimes, he does each eye in different colors, so they don't match.

Then I go out to the kitchen, to the little round wooden table with the mismatched Goodwill chairs, and have my cereal. Grampie eats oatmeal with brown sugar. He has gray hair that used to be chocolate brown, and brilliant blue eyes that hide behind his reading glasses. He's always been on the skinny side, but he's developed a gut since he stopped working. His retirement uniform is a pair of Carhartt pants and a white tee. His voice is scratchy from smoking for so many years.

We always tell each other to have a good day, and then I go outside and jump on my bike.

Gates High School is a cage full of zombie kids. I'm forced to go in there every day and pretend to be one of them. But even being the artistic rebel girl is a role I've gotten sick of.

It's like someone has to be the outsider, and it's me, but most of these people don't really know that I'm not solely defined by pink hair and rainbow eye shadow.

Thank the Goddess for Nick, who waits for me every morning at the door by the cafeteria. He knows what my home is like, what my heart is like.

Let's get one thing absolutely clear: I am not a girl who thinks that high school is the best time of my life. My real life hasn't actually started yet. I can't wait to get out of here.

My hair defined me on the first day of high school. It was dark brown with blue bangs. On my neck I had a Sharpie rose tattoo, which took me hours to do in the mirror.

That first day of school, someone wrote "freak" on my

8

homeroom desk while I was in the hallway and the teacher was busy handing out locker assignments.

At my private middle school, Ocean Tides, I hadn't felt like a freak. I hadn't been bored, either. We'd all been encouraged to be who we felt like being. I thought that was normal. I thought everyone had talents and interests and points of view. My Ocean Tides pal Holly is all about music the way I'm all about art.

So when I saw that word, as much as it burned me— and it did—I was thankful for it. It meant they knew I was different.

I'd rather be a freak than blend into this world, where everyone goes around acting as if it's normal to all be the same.

A lot of people are just spinning time. Just wasting it. I'm trying to live.

Two

Nick has mastered this way of standing so that it looks like he's smoking, but he's not. Real chilled out.

After I lock my bike to the crowded rack, I walk up to him. "Do we really have to go in there? When will the torture end?"

"June, two years from now," he says, meaning graduation. As he shifts his weight, he exhales imaginary smoke.

"Yeah, but then what?"

We walk into school.

"Then we'll be free," Nick says.

But I want to be free now. Why not? What's holding us back?

"Hope so," I say. "At least it's Friday."

We have a few minutes, so we stand there looking around. I watch the yearbook photographer, a junior in a Gates High sweatshirt, as she circulates. A group of girls walking toward us all stop and put their arms around each other. For the second that they're posing, they look really happy. Then the moment's over and they just look bored.

I take Nick's hand and we walk inside. The hallway is our runway and people notice my new hair. They're used to it changing, but they still look.

The yearbook photographer snaps a couple of shots. I curtsy to her before giving Nick a hug and heading into homeroom.

After school, Nick and I hang out in my garage, where I have a little art studio and Grampie keeps his Chevy. Nick sits cross-legged on my drop cloth with his sketchbook, playing around with new comic characters. He's trying to draw this guy who's like a cross between Prince Charming and an outlaw. "If I can get him right, I might start another strip."

"Cool." I stand at my easel and paint cherry blossoms on a bent branch. There's this scene in my head. A memory? A dream? Cherry blossoms float all around me as I lie flat on my back on the sidewalk. Pink petals swirling through the blue-sky air, a surreal, fantastic snowstorm.

Nick works. I work. This is so much better than school. Eventually, we head inside for burritos and to get ready for the Fremont Art Walk.

Mom and Grampie are already at the table eating dinner: tuna fish sandwiches.

"You two are going to turn into burritos," Mom says as I pop them into the microwave and Nick pours us lemonade.

"There are worse things to turn into," I say.

Nick says, "At my house, we have all these fancy-pants preprepared gourmet meals. Microwaves were made for things like burritos. Not shrimp in a delicate wine sauce. These burritos keep me sane."

"Popcorn," Grampie says.

Nick and I sit down. "Popcorn?" I ask.

"Popcorn was the first thing to be cooked in a microwave. By a guy named Percy Spencer and his team, in 1945. The second thing they cooked was an egg, which exploded into one of their faces." Grampie takes a bite of tuna.

Nick looks impressed. "No wonder you're so good at those crosswords, Mr. Almond."

"I keep telling you," I say. "Grampie is a genius."

Mom nods. "Popcorn sounds good tonight. Have some with our movie later, Dad?"

"Air-popped," Grampie says. "Nothing good comes out of microwaves."

"I beg to differ," I say, taking out the burritos.

We all eat, and it feels like the night will be just right.

Then I put on the shortest of my three black minis and a black tank. A constellation of silver glitter stars on my black bra peeks out.

Nick pops into my room and looks at my wrist string. "Still blue. Good."

Blue is second only to purple, the best.

He shakes an eyeliner brush at me and I sit down at the desk chair.

"I really, really hope you decide to stick with this."

"With what?"

"Makeup."

"Like, for a career?" He roots around in my toolbox-style case.

"You'd do the most fabulous celebrities. Only the quirky ones."

"Oh, of course. Including my world-famous friend, Vanessa Almond . . ."

"Of course!"

"Remind me. What are you famous for again?"

"Art!"

I close my eyes and let him create a new face for me.

What would it be like to use a living canvas for more than makeup? To color someone's whole body?

When Nick's done, I look pretty and bright. Not too wild. Intense colors, but no lightning bolts or sparkles. Just deep purple on the eyelids and super-black lashes. Pale lips. Rosy cheeks.

"Okay?" he asks.

"Perfect."

He closes up the box and walks out to the family room. Grampie starts talking to him about the Mariners game, how many outs.

I wiggle into and zip up my favorite-Christmas-present white twenty-eye Doc Martens. Zippers are a wonderful invention.

In the family room, Nick is hovering behind Grampie, who's on the couch with a crossword puzzle on his lap, a pen in his hand, and the game on across the room.

Grampie says, "Nick, sit down."

"I would, Mr. Almond, but we're going to the Fremont Art Walk tonight."

"And here I am, being lazy on the couch."

"But still using that amazing brain of yours, I see," Nick says.

Grampie holds up his crossword. "What's an eight-letter word for a baseball team who just can't get it together?"

"No idea."

"Ha! *Mariners.*" I walk up next to the couch.

"Attagirl."

"He asks me that every time he watches a game," I tell Nick.

I can't help but think that lately Grampie looks like a little old man. He's retired, and he's obviously the grandfather of a teenager, but when did he start looking old? And smaller? He's grayer. Not just his steel-wool hair, but his skin, too. He moves more slowly.

There's a photo of him and my grandmother that sits on the mantel. It's how I picture him in all the days before I was born, before even my mom was born. Grampie stands, laughing as she strikes a pose; she's sitting on the hood of his Chevy, the one that still lives in our garage.

My grandmother was a beautiful woman, and this is by far my favorite photo of her. She's so full of life. She radiates energy, you can tell just by looking.

"Nicolai says you're off to Fremont for the art walk," Grampie says.

"Yep," I say. "We're meeting up with Holly. I'll be back by eleven."

"I'll tell your mother."

"Where is she, anyway?" I ask.

As if on cue, Mom walks out of her room and slumps down next to Grampie, looking just as tired as he does. "Right here."

Mom works so hard at the docks. She insists on being called a *longshoreman*. She deserves to sit behind a cushy desk in some office filing her nails and listening to the radio, instead of checking in the cargo coming off boats and into Ballard. Instead of worrying about manifests, and stacking crates, and sometimes driving the forklift. She should get to take it easy.

Whenever I try to talk to her about that, she says how well the docks pay, and then I clam up because I know that her having me is the reason she doesn't have the education to get other good-paying jobs.

"I'll never understand why you would rather sit on the couch than get out there on the weekends," I say.

"Talk to me after you've been out there working for fifteen years," Mom says. One of her favorite lines.

"Grampie did it for almost fifty years. And he still has a social life."

He keeps his head down, as he always does when this line of conversation comes up. Nick does too.

"I'm happy, Vanessa. I'm fine."

"You haven't even had a date in months and months, Mom. The docks are your whole life."

Mom just shakes her head.

Nick tugs on my arm.

I kiss Grampie's cheek, grab my faux-leather motorcycle jacket, and head out. I decide to try to live enough life for both me and my mom.

Nick skips ahead, oblivious to the fact that anyone's even aware of him. He doesn't know it, but I admire that about him. He lives moment by moment.

I walk behind him, let him shine.

In Ballard, there's salt in the air, just a hint. You know the water's not far away, and you know that fish are swimming out there, and that this world is not a new world. It's as old as the ocean and everything in it.

Our street is lined with small shingled houses and messy yards, tulips in every garden, though they're not in bloom quite yet, and cherry trees near the sidewalk. Those trees will burst into color soon. When they do, the city will feel fresh.

With all that salt from Puget Sound in the air, Ballard can feel worn-in. Comfy, but not squeaky clean. It's a fantastic place to call home.

Nick's house is three blocks away from mine and farther from the stores, much bigger than my house. When they moved here a few years ago, his parents tore down the little house on their lot to build this ultramodern thing that looks like a bank or a mini office building.

My family has lived in the same tiny house since Grampie was a boy. He grew up there. Grampie fixed up the basement when I was twelve, to give Mom and me more space.

My grandmother was already gone by the time I was born. We keep all the photos of her on the fireplace mantel. I think Mom looks a lot like her, but I don't see myself in her. Mom and Grampie say my birth was the thing in the universe that balanced out her death. I like the idea. Not that she's gone, but that I somehow make up for her death a little.

The bus stop is at the corner of Twenty-Sixth, just a couple of blocks back from Market Street, where Ballard stops being residential and starts being citylike.

Nick gets there first, and when I join him he says, "I love Fridays."

"Me too." I put my arm around him, and we stand there looking like two wild teenagers waiting for something to happen. Something more than a bus showing up, headed toward Fremont.

But sometimes, a bus and your neon friend are enough.

"I'm glad you're getting to know Holly," I say as we get off the bus across the street from Caffe Ladro, our first stop on the art walk.

"She's a sweetheart." It was Holly's sweetness that made us into friends the first week of sixth grade. I was terrified to talk to anyone, but Holly marched right up to me during "nature exploration"—Ocean Tides Middle School code for "recess"—to ask if I wanted to build fairy houses with her.

Holly lives in Fremont—right next to Ballard but with a different vibe, less about the water and more about creativity and Thai food. Her house is taller than mine, but still shingled. Her yard is even tinier than mine, her house closer to the road.

Holly practices the cello from six until eight every

night, even Friday and Saturday. Even on the days when she's got organized practice after school and has already played for two hours. Practice makes perfect, and Holly's driven; she doesn't want to accept less than perfect when it comes to her music.

We'll meet up with her right after Ladro. We have just enough time to pop in.

We cross the busy street in the dying light of spring-time. I catch a whiff of Indian spices from the restaurant by the bus stop.

"Wonder who's exhibiting this month," Nick says, holding the door for me. As if we'll know the artist. An exhibiting artist wants nothing to do with two high school kids.

Even if I'm the best artist at school, I'm nothing out here in the real world.

There's a long line for coffee, and the shop is pretty crowded, people mingling and eating free snacks. When I see the photos on the wall, I realize that we do know the artist.

It's Jewel. The reason my insides are twisty. The cause of my one stint with the black string. He's a high school sophomore, like me. But he has this show. And I have . . . what?

"Let's just go meet Holly," I say.

Nick doesn't question. He can radar that I'm uncom-fortable.

Nick and I weren't that close yet when Jewel mashed my heart into my toes last fall. In fact, less time with Jewel was the start of more time with Nick. Friend-dating is so much easier than dating-dating.

"Sure," he says. "Let's go."

I want to. But I don't turn to leave.

Jewel's biting into a cookie, standing in a huddle with his overalls-wearing mom, and with Alice Davis, whose ponytail looks as perfect as ever, and her folks, who are wearing conservationist tees I know they screen-printed themselves. Alice wears one too. Hers and her mom's have a tree with roots, and her dad's has a dolphin. Back when Alice and I were in elementary school, before I went to Ocean Tides, Alice gave me one about saving bees. I wore it forever.

She and I have a tiny friendship, a sort of understanding or respect, because we were friends as kids. But lately, due to Jewel, our good thoughts and feelings about each other are this cactus we're both afraid to touch.

Jewel looks to see who Mr. Davis is waving at. His eyes—his amazing eyes that seek and find beauty in every little thing—glint as he locks on me. I feel zapped. As if there's light, sound, and *this*. Jewel's electric gaze.

Alice notices me. She gives me that look. The one she's been giving me since the fall, simultaneously sweet and kind of cruel, because we both know Jewel wants her and not me. She has him. She gets to be happy about that. And I get nothing.

Jewel smiles. My hand rises as if I'm a marionette, and I manage to wiggle my fingers.

I am my own puppet master.

I just hope no one else can see how those strings are the only things keeping me standing and smiling.

Three

I can't leave now that they've seen me. I would be running.

I take Nick's hand and lead him to the snack table, where there's raspberry fizzy water for us youngsters. I'm tempted to sneak some white wine instead. Escape.

Nick drops my hand and pours us each a paper cup of the fizz, and we look at the work on the walls. I keep my back to Jewel, but it's like he's true north to my body's compass. I sense where he is.

I try to focus on the moment, the way Nick can. Breathe. Sip.

The first photo we check out is of the Fremont Troll, a

sculpture that lives near Jewel's house. It's all big and creepy and weird. That's what he loves about it. Me too. This photo is a close-up of the troll's eye, a hubcap.

We drift to another photo. A snail's head. Black-and-white.

There's something gorgeous in that snail. I stare.

"Wishing you had a shell to hide in?" Nick asks.

"That would be nice."

"Come on," he says. "You don't cower."

He's right. "I'm gonna go say hi."

As I step toward Jewel, he breaks from his group to meet me. If I could fall into his arms right here, I would. In front of everyone. In front of Alice.

"Nice stuff," I say.

"Glad you like it," he says. "Your hair looks awesome. Doing the walk tonight?"

I touch my hair without wanting to. Smile. He knows I do the walk every month. We've done it together. I nod. "And meeting a friend."

He knows Nick is gay, but maybe he'll think the friend is another guy. Maybe he'll think I've fallen for someone else.

"Gotcha," he says. "Thanks for stopping by. Have a good night."

"I will." I turn and go out the door with Nick.

It kills me that no night without Jewel will ever be as good as the few we spent together.

Nick and I get to the gelato shop before Holly. I send him in to grab a table while I wait for her outside, leaning against the brick building and watching the neighborhood breathe.

Lots of people are out tonight, strolling with dogs, doing the art walk, browsing the shops, eating at the Thai restaurants, and starting to crowd the bars. The sun is low, but the sky's not completely night-black. Some blue survives.

I relax to the music of car engines and car tires and car doors as people get out and join the night. I don't know how I'd ever survive living anywhere but the city. Everywhere else is too quiet. In the country, if you stop to think about a boy who broke your heart, you might never get jolted back into life.

Headlights swim past. People laugh. A dog barks. I stand straight: Girl Waiting for a Friend. Not Girl with a Mashed Heart.

Here comes Holly, bouncing. The girl is a true light. She's got long blond hair and big blue eyes. She's as perfectly gorgeous as the cliché, classically beautiful and tall in a flowery skirt and a ruffly yellow top under her denim jacket. If she went to public school with me instead of Saint Agatha's, she'd probably be prom queen.

Her school doesn't have a prom, let alone a queen. Her

mother thinks dressing her in a uniform and forcing her out of the sight line of boys will keep her pure or something. It's kind of working. Girl is innocent.

She's the only person from Ocean Tides I still hang out with on a regular basis; we'll always be tight at the core.

"Love the pink!" She gives me a hug.

There's definitely something to be said for the Ocean Tides brand of hippiedom, where we got to go skiing Fridays in the winter and cook lunch for ourselves whenever we wanted, with an oven and using real knives, and where we were encouraged to spend time and energy on the things we were naturally drawn to.

I bet I wouldn't know anything about Jackson Pollock or Duchamp or modern art if not for Ocean Tides. Holly spent half of middle school in the music room with her cello.

I often wonder how much more free I'd feel if there had been a high school version of our school.

I squeeze her.

Pulling back, she says, "I only have an hour."

"Inside, pronto."

We find Nick sitting with a coffee at the table by the back window, perfect for people-watching. Holly waves at him, and he lifts his cup.

We wait behind a family with three kids who can't make up their minds.

"I'm feeling chocolate tonight," I say.

"Me too."

"So how was your week?"

A magazine-ready grin stretches across her face.

"What's up?"

"Last night was practice for the city youth orchestra. . . ."

Holly's in three different orchestras, but this smile is so not about the cello.

"A guy?"

"I'm totally crushing."

"Sweet!" I say. "Tell me."

"His name's Wilson. . . ."

The family's done paying, and the old guy who owns the gelato shop is standing there in his black T-shirt and orange apron, holding little pink sample spoons. We usually try a few flavors—Holly always dares me to try the weird ones, like rose and persimmon—but tonight's quick.

"Medium chocolate, please," I say.

"Make it two."

We go sit with Nick with our scoops.

Nick opens his mouth, but I say, "Wait! Holly's telling us about a boy."

She's still sparkling. "Wilson. He plays violin. So good. And so adorable! Super-short hair. Cute Harry Potter glasses. And he wears this T-shirt that looks like a Boy Scout shirt."

"Ironically or earnestly?" I ask.

Nick says, "I know that guy. He's in my gym class. He's a junior."

"Wait," I say. "Do I know him?"

"Wilson! Brown hair?" Holly asks. "Dimples? The glasses?"

"You've seen him around, I'm sure," Nick says.

"Gah!" I don't remember him. "I'll have to keep an eye out."

"I can't believe this! I knew he went to public school, but not where. Nessie, why don't you come to our concert next week? I promise it won't be too boring," Holly says. "You too, Nick. It's on Friday."

"Not sure," Nick says. "That's the start of Superhero Origins Weekend on the SyFy channel. I want to check out the movie lineup."

"Text me the details," I say. "I'd love to go."

Nick's got a far-off look. "Small city," he says.

"A nice city, too, but tell that to my mother," Holly says. "To hear her tell it, we live at the crossroads of Hades and Gotham. Evil."

"Oh, your mom isn't that bad."

"She can be," Holly says.

"Besides, small places can be evil," Nick says.

"For example, Gates High," I throw in.

"Not to mention Saint Agatha's," Holly says.

"I'm sure," Nick says, with a sparkle in his own eye.

"All those girls. Not a single prospect in sight for any of us. Real tragedy."

"As if we have any prospects now," I say. "Except for Holly and her Wilson."

"My Wilson. I wish."

Nick doesn't say anything. He's got this thing about how he won't date until college, or after. He's not the only guy at school who's out, but he's not into any of the others. He says they're boring.

"So, what do you have going on this weekend?" Holly asks.

"Nada mucho," Nick says.

"I've got my interview tomorrow," I say. "You guys. Imagine—it would be perfect. My first job. In the art store I've loved my whole life. I'd get a discount on all those beautiful supplies. I could make cash *and* hang out at Palette."

This job would be the first step to my dream: the true life of an artist in the real world.

"You'll get it," Holly says.

"I hope so, because Palette's the only place I want to work, and I need to start earning some cash. I want to save for my tattoo." They don't know how much I want to help Mom with bills, too. So she can work a little less and live a little more.

"Like I said. Don't worry," Holly says. "A tattoo . . . Not me. My parents would freak."

"Grampie has one. A sockeye salmon on his bicep. So he can't complain."

Nick asks, "What about your mom, though?"

"We've talked about it. She doesn't like the idea, but what's she gonna do?" I shrug as I lick my spoon.

They exchange a look. Holly says, "Um, say no? Ground you?"

"I told her I'll wait till I'm eighteen, but I'm not sure I can."

"I'm going with you when you get it." Nick's excited now.

"Oh, me too!"

"You are both cordially invited."

Holly and I enjoy our gelato, Nick sips his coffee, and I savor this window of time: there's art waiting to be seen, I'm with my friends, love's on the horizon, and maybe a dream job, too.

I've managed to push my mashed heart far away from my brain, although I'm not sure it's a good idea to try and forget a thing like that.

After Holly heads home, Nick and I art-walk for another hour. The glass studio has a show of huge paintings, all at least seven feet tall and wide, abstracts with blues and greens. They look alive. They look as if they're breathing.

"Kind of like Pollock," I say.

"Him again?" Nick knows I really love Jackson Pollock. "Will you ever get over that guy?"

"Probably not. He's pretty much perfect."

"Except for the extreme alcoholism and the whole being dead thing."

"Yeah, except for that."

We keep looking around, and I realize these paintings aren't actually much like Pollock's work. They're much more thought out. Possibly too organized.

The artist is there, holding hands with his boyfriend.

I nod toward them. "No one's looking at them weird or anything."

"What's your point?"

"We live in a city that accepts two dudes holding hands. Doesn't that make you feel good?"

"Sure," he says. He turns to look at a painting in shades of turquoise.

"That's it?"

"What else do you want me to say?"

"I want you to say why you refuse to ever tell me who you like, or to ask anyone out. There's no reason you can't have a crush just like Holly. You could meet someone online, I bet. And there are, like, groups who do this kind of thing. Mingling. Art nights. Game nights. Bowling."

"Bowling?" he says. "Look, this is hard to explain to you because you're . . . normal?"

I put out my arms like airplane wings. "Look normal?"

"Okay, but you're straight. And that's all you really need."

"For what?"

"For . . . I don't know. For a certain comfort level. To be able to crush-gush over gelato."

"But that's just what I'm saying. Holly and I don't care. The general public doesn't care. You can gush!"

"The thing, I think, is that once people know you're gay, they can't look at you and not think about sex."

"But you don't have sex. That's my point."

"Yeah, and I won't until I'm away from people who knew me as a kid. Away from my parents. Until I'm in a place where sexuality is expected."

"What place is that?"

"College, I guess."

I snort. "Yeah, no one has sex before college."

"I'm serious. I'm waiting till I'm ready. And I'm not ready now. For any of it."

"But when I looked at those guys, I didn't think about them having sex. I just thought they were adorable."

"Are you in the habit of envisioning the sex lives of your elders?"

I think about it. "No."

"See?"

"But I'm not in the habit of envisioning the sex lives of anyone." Except Jewel and Alice. I wonder . . .

31

"But if people come across two high school guys holding hands, they just see them as these sexual deviants and nothing else."

"Um, I doubt it."

"Well, I'm not ready to test your doubt. I'm fine on my own."

The shop is closing, so we head out to the sidewalk. I hold Nick's hand.

"This conversation is over for now," I say. "But not for good."

We ride the bus to the stop by his house.

He bids me good night, with a bow and a flourish.

Jewel encounter and semi-disagreement with Nick aside, it was a decent night out.

When I get home, I open the front door to find Mom cuddled up on the couch with a blanket, reading a thick mystery. She's wearing her at-home sweats, as opposed to her at-work sweats. The work ones smell like the docks, grimy and fishy. The home ones smell like rain-scent fabric softener. She uses too much of that stuff. I'm glad to do my own laundry.

Airport-style novels are to my mom what I suppose bubble baths are to some people: a way to decompress and escape.

She tosses her book on the coffee table as soon as I shut the door.

I drop my jacket in the tiny entryway, where the beige linoleum tiles mash up against the ancient green shag rug.

I sit down at the other end of the couch, take off my boots, grab a corner of her blanket, and curl up, our feet touching.

"How was your night?" I ask her.

"Fine." Her curly hair is half out of its ponytail. She's only thirty-four, but she looks older. She looks so tired. She works so hard.

I have more of a life than my mother. That must be depressing for her.

"Tell me about the book."

She does, and sitting there with her is the perfect way to end a night. Maybe Nick's right, I think. Everything doesn't have to happen right this second.

Four

It's interview day.

After I shower, I tie a blue string around my wrist and dress in my dark purple netty top with the V, a shiny black tank, and shortish black pleated skirt, full like a cheerleader skirt. Then, my hot pink fishnets—which make the cheerleader thing ironic and which are awesome because they match my hair and it's finally warm enough to wear them.

I consider doing something all-out with my makeup, like using glitter or drawing on liner like cat eyes. Black lipstick? But I just keep it simple—dark purple on the eyelids, soft pink lips. More professional.

Mom's at the kitchen table with her tea. She barely looks up as I get my cereal before she says, "That outfit is not appropriate for a sixteen-year-old." She likes to pretend she's strict.

"I'm not changing."

She catches my eye. She looks like a painting as the steam from her tea rises in front of her face.

We've had this discussion before. It's not about my hair. Mom doesn't mind if I dress "a little bit wild" and "colorfully" but she "will not put up with too sexy."

"It's almost summer, Mom. This is totally appropriate."

She's still got her gaze on me as I pour Cheerios and milk. "Where are you going, anyway?"

"I have my interview at Palette today. For the job?"

She sips tea. I can practically see her decide to not make me change my clothes. She's weighed the scales. Job is a bigger deal than skirt. She knows I'll feel more like myself if I dress the way I want. "I want your homework finished by the time I get back from the docks tonight."

Her working on Saturdays is a huge part of why I want this job. If I can at least pay my own phone bill and buy my own art supplies, she might be able to give up her extra workday. Then she could get an actual life.

"No problem."

* * *

I jump on my bicycle. This skirt is plenty loose enough to bike.

My ride is an old three-speed beach cruiser, very sixties. It's perfect for getting around Ballard, and to and from school.

I pass my bus stop. On Market Street, I turn left. Just a few more blocks.

Palette is in the main strip of the neighborhood, near a movie theater, a bakery, and a crowded skate park. Cobblestones and brick buildings.

I open the door, a cheery look plastered on my face. Palette is empty.

I walk through the aisles, over the cement floor splattered with a rainbow of dry paint drips. The ceiling is high, like a warehouse, and the messy floor makes me feel as if I'm in a painter's studio. The shelves are metal.

I've been coming here since I was a kid. In here, time doesn't exist. I'd happily stay forever. It's got everything I need to survive. Even caffeine.

Oscar is the owner. He looks too young to own anything but an attitude—except that he's prematurely balding, so he shaves his head. He comes out from the back room, up to the long counter with the register.

"Hey," he says. "Vanessa, right?"

"That's me." I reach across the counter to shake his hand. It feels odd because I already know who he is.

"I've seen you around here," he says. "Glad you applied for the job." He's kind of Zen, which is a phase I went through a few months ago. He has this aura of sweetness, though he wears real tough-guy stuff, plain black tees tight to his muscled body. I'm in love with his pretty tattoos, two full sleeves of trees and vines. Green leaves. A few purple berries.

Mom should study him as an example of someone who dresses kind of edgy but is clearly a good and responsible person.

"Yep," I say. "It's my favorite store, actually."

He grins. "That's what I like to hear." He gestures at the couch beside the espresso bar. "Let's sit."

I take a seat, as ladylike as I can, on the orange couch with hot pink flowers. I've always wondered whose aunt Madge must've kicked the bucket for the store to inherit this thing.

Oscar flops down at the other end, resting his back on the armrest, his steel-toe boots on the couch, knees in the air.

"I'm looking to hire someone to help out at our busiest shifts. Open-to-close on Saturdays, for sure. Maybe we can add some short evening shifts, too. A good chance for someone your age to make some pocket money. Plus, thirty percent off everything we sell. And free coffee."

"Awesome." Money earned, and money saved.

"So, what makes Palette your favorite store?"

"Well, it's a useful place." I've never quite put these ideas into words before. "Palette is a place where you come to buy something you need, because you have a project you want to do. Something worth it. And even more than that. Palette's a place where you can come to be inspired, even."

He widens his eyes. "Wow. Right. So, you're an artist, then?"

"Yeah," I say. I feel so young, sitting here, begging for a job. "I mean, really. Art is pretty much the most important thing to me."

He looks like he's expecting more, so I say, "And I'm good at it." I hope he doesn't ask for more, because I doubt that straight As in Mr. Smith's workshop would hold much weight here. "I mean, people seem to like my stuff. My work." That sounds more official, right?

Should I mention first place in the school art show last fall? Nah.

"Interesting," he says. "But really, what's most important in this job is that you show up on time, you're one hundred percent reliable, professional and honest, you do a neat and careful job when you're stocking, you master the workings of our ancient register system, and you listen to whatever Maye says about the espresso bar. Sound like you're up to all that?"

"Definitely. Sounds good to me." The vintage-style mint green espresso machine looks so inviting.

"What happened to the coffee guy with the Mohawk?" He skimps on the whipped cream. I'd love to get my hands on that nozzle.

"He moved."

"So I'll have to fill the position of Palette Employee with Funky Hair," I say. "Don't worry about me moving on or being too busy on the weekends or anything."

He smiles. "This would be your first job?"

I nod. "Technically, but I'm used to working really hard. School, and art, and all. I hope that I could add more hours in the summer. I really want to start earning money."

"If all goes well, that should be doable," he says. "I've got a few other people to talk to today. I'll call you soon with a decision?"

He says it like a question, so as he stands up, I stand and say, "That'd be great."

I'm about to shake Oscar's hand again when a tall blond guy glides up to the front door on a long skateboard, wearing sandals, perfect-fitting jeans, and a T-shirt, as if it's the middle of summer. He steps off the board, grabs it, and comes into the shop. His hair is almost white. It flops in front of his eyes. He's tan. It's like he just stepped out of Hawaii.

"Hey, James," Oscar calls out.

"Yo." James has a camera around his neck, just like Jewel usually does. He's nineteen or twenty.

James sits on the couch. "Maye in? I've got official business with her."

I really want to hear what he has to say, but I know that's my cue to exit. I paste on my most responsible smile. "Thanks, Oscar. Love the new easels," I say. "The bamboo ones. I, like, covet them."

Then I pretty much run away. *I covet your easels?* That was the best last line I could think of? And in front of Blond, James Blond?

How childish. Who would hire a child?

I can only hope that Oscar would.

As I pedal up to the house, Mom is just getting out of her old Jeep with groceries. I help her unload in the kitchen. She bought stuff for lasagna, Grampie's favorite. She heads to her room for a nap before her Saturday late shift.

I look at my desk. No. No homework on a Saturday. That's what Sunday night is for.

I would call Holly, but I know she locked herself in for the day to practice for her big concert.

I text Nick. He's having "family day," which is hilarious. You can practically see the quotes around those two words when he texts back . . . family day is his parents' way of making up for the fact that they only spend that one

40

night a month together. His parents ignore him until this one day when they all go to the movies—they pick action flicks or comedies, anything without real emotion that they might be tempted to discuss later—and out to dinner, where his parents talk about their jobs and Nick counts down the minutes until he can get home to catch up on reality TV on the DVR.

So. Homework on a Saturday might not be that bad after all. It'll free up my Sunday. And I'll be doing what Mom asked this morning.

I throw on my splattered T-shirt dress, set up my books on the kitchen table, and dig into Spanish. Grampie sits across from me with his crossword puzzle, sipping lemonade. It's kind of peaceful.

Mom comes in, ready for work.

"Heading out?" Grampie asks her.

"In a minute," she says. She grabs a banana from the bowl on the counter and sits with us to eat it.

"Nice dinner," I say. Oops. It's not her fault that she doesn't have time for a real meal. "I mean, want some peanut butter? For protein?"

Grampie shoots me a look that means something like *Give it up*. Then he takes his puzzle. "See you in the morning, darlin'." He kisses Mom and heads down to his room. I love it when he calls her that.

"Bye, Dad." She turns her attention back to me. "I can take care of myself, Nessie."

"I know. Sorry. I just don't like to see you so rushy-rushy all the time."

"That's life, is all. Gotta work." She folds up the banana peels into a little package.

"Well, I hope I get my job so I can help out a little. Maybe you can stop working Saturday nights."

I see something shift in Mom's face. She swallows. "You don't have to worry about bills. That's what I'm here for. And Paul's been sending some money."

"I don't remember the last time I actually heard from Paul." I doubt he even thinks of me as a real person. I'm more like this abstract thing that happened to him when he was barely older than I am now. "I can't imagine a guy my age with a baby."

"Funny," Mom says, "neither can I. But I remember what it was like to be a young mom. Pushing you in your stroller. People at the grocery store assumed I was your babysitter."

"Did you feel like my babysitter?"

"Nessie, I stopped feeling like a kid the moment you were born." She looks at the microwave clock. "Gotta go."

And she's off.

I don't like to think about Paul, so I force myself to read a fake menu in my book, decoding *huevos* and *leche*.

Soon enough, I'm finished.

I do think about Paul some more, and how Grampie took over what he should have been doing. I get the sketchbook from my bag and start to draw a scene that's been in my head for years . . . Grampie's face as he watched me ride a bike on my own for the first time. He's the one who taught me. He was lit up.

When I'm finished sketching, it's still pretty early, so I call Holly.

"Nessie!"

"Yo. Are you practicing?"

"Just finished."

"Come over?"

"Sure."

A little while later, we're watching some old monster movie and eating ice cream on the couch, just the way I sat with Mom last night.

I put my feet against hers. "You know, you're part of my family."

"Aw. You too. Why so mushy?"

"Just thinking about that stuff lately, I guess."

"Like what?"

"How weird life is. You know?"

"I think so."

"My mom said she grew up when I was born. I feel as if I'm waiting for my real life to start. Do you ever feel like that?"

Someone screams on the TV. I turn down the volume. "Yeah. In a way." She puts her bowl on the coffee table. "I mean, I'm busy with music. It kind of is my life."

"Yeah. And I have art. But is that what really defines my life?"

"I think you know yourself better than you think you do, Vanessa."

"You think I'm self-aware?"

"Duh. More than anyone else. You're so Vanessa. It's like they said at Ocean Tides. 'Follow your bliss.' You do that."

"How do you mean?"

"I mean, look at you! A walking piece of art."

I beam. "Thanks, Holly. And you're a walking piece of music." She raises her eyebrows. "Or something. You're really talented, and you work so hard."

I don't say what I think next: *But I don't*. I don't really try very hard at anything. Art is natural for me. I've never pushed my boundaries.

But I want to. I want to work as hard at art as Holly does with her music, and do something big.

I turn the volume back up and she and I watch this whole bunch of picnickers by a lake get chomped by a monster that's part alligator, part zombie.

After that, we take turns reading to each other from Mom's mystery.

Eventually, Holly calls home and asks if she can stay. We set up blankets on the floor next to my bed and have a slumber party.

44

It feels so good to have her here. Holly falls asleep and I listen to her breathing.

I stare at the ceiling, trying to keep myself in the moment.

Mom gets home around two in the morning. When I hear the front door open and close, I'm tempted to go out to the family room to share the calm middle-of-the-night with her.

Instead, I finally drift off to sleep.

Five

Holly's folding the blankets when I wake up on Sunday.

"How'd you sleep?"

"I dreamed about Mozart."

"That's good, right?"

"That's very, very good."

"Great. I don't remember what I dreamed. I don't think I did."

She puts the blankets on the foot of my bed. "People dream every night. We just don't always remember."

Mom pokes her head in. "I thought I saw your shoes, Miss Holly."

"Hi, Ms. Almond. Yeah, I stayed over. Hope you don't mind."

"Of course I don't mind. Our home is your home."

"Hey, Mom?"

"Yeah?"

"I want to make pancakes, okay?"

"Oh, Nessie. I don't know if I have the energy. Would cereal be okay?"

"No, I'm not asking you to make pancakes. I want to make them. For you and Grampie and Holly."

My mom's face lights up. Like pancakes are a big gift.

I tell her, "Go read." Holly helps me in the kitchen.

Most of my strange little family is around one table. Only Nick is missing.

Mom tells us about her friend Mindy's four-year-old girl, how they drew princesses together. I'd love to draw with my mom again.

"You used to draw your princesses with fangs," Grampie says to me.

Holly nearly spits out her orange juice. "Seriously?"

"Abso-snootly. She would do the crowns and the big poufy gowns. And then the princess would get her fangs." Grampie looks as if he can see it now. I'm still four years old, sitting across this table from him.

"Why do I feel like the fangs might've been your influence, Grampie?"

"I never was one for the ordinary," he says. "You've got me there. But the fangs were your own creation."

We all laugh, finish our pancakes, talking.

A perfect breakfast.

When Holly leaves, I head out to the garage.

Grampie's working on his Chevy. Mom parks her Jeep out on the street so that he can keep his classic beauty safe and dry in here. He barely drives it. It's kind of like his pet.

I have a canvas out here that I've been painting for months, layer after layer. I paint something—Grampie bent over the engine of the Chevy, a teacup, Mom's face—and then I paint it black. Then prime it white. Start over.

Kind of like I do with my hair.

Today, I'm using the black to erase my cherry blossom from Friday.

Soon there will be actual cherry blossoms in bloom, right outside, lining the streets of Ballard. The buds are filling up. Any day, they'll burst and be the most beautiful color.

My cell buzzes when my canvas is almost completely black. Grampie went inside at some point, and I didn't even notice. I was zoning. I'm unsettled when I realize I didn't notice him go, but the thought is fleeting.

I plop my brush on the drop sheet and check the phone. A number I don't recognize.

"Hello?"

"Vanessa. Oscar, Palette."

"Hey." Good news? It's so fast. If it was a no, he probably wouldn't be calling to tell me. Unless that's exactly why he's calling.

"So, those other two applicants were both no-shows."

"Seriously? How lame of them." Why would anyone bother to apply for a job and then not show for the interview?

"Yeah. Well, I like you anyway. Can you start next Saturday? Ten a.m.?"

"Absolutely."

"Great, Vanessa. See you then!"

"I'm so excited. Thank you, Oscar!"

My heart is pumping fast.

I call Holly; I call Nick. They're both psyched.

I go to the back door and see Grampie and Mom sitting at the table. They look up from their tuna melts as I open the door. I'm surprised by how glad I am to see them sitting there like that.

"I got the job!"

Grampie raises his sandwich in celebration. "Hey, that's great. My working girl."

I smile at him. Then I look at Mom, who has little creases near her eyes. She's worried, but trying not to show it. "I hope this will be good for you."

"I know it will be." I do. A real-world job. Where I will totally reinvent myself. "And I'll meet new people, and get a discount."

"Sounds good, Nessie," Grampie says, but Mom still has that crease.

"It's fine, Mom. I want to work."

Grampie gets up and puts his plate in the sink, then heads down to his room. Guess he's not all that interested. Or he's trying to stay out of our way.

I sit down across from her. "Why shouldn't I have a job? What's bothering you about it?"

She pushes her plate away. I think she might cry. I hold my breath. There must be something big she wants to say.

"I feel like I grew up really fast."

I'm still barely breathing. "Because of me."

"Because I got pregnant and started to get ready for a baby and then your grandmother died. I had to grow up fast and early. Support us. You don't have to do that."

My heart breaks a little every time I remember that she gave up so much of her life to raise me. She was only a few months older than I am now.

"You don't have to do this. Have fun. Join clubs, stuff like that."

She wants me to stay a little girl? Tough luck. "Clubs? No way."

She nods. "Maybe school clubs are stupid, but all I'm saying is you don't need to do this for us. We're okay."

"I get that, Mom. This is not a big deal. It'll be fun. Really interesting. It's not like I'm setting out to work at the docks. I'm working in art. I thought you'd be happy."

"I just want to be sure you have time to focus on your art and your schoolwork. Setting yourself up for later."

"Are you talking about college?"

"College, yes. Art school, maybe. But finishing high school, doing well, and enjoying this time of your life. You're only a sophomore."

"Mom. This is a way for me to spend time living my real life. I'm ready for responsibility." I don't get it. I'm not doing anything wrong. "I'll always be your kid. Okay?"

"Sure, Nessie! Of course you will." Something shifts in her face. We're done talking. "Garden time for me!"

I watch her go, and I want to follow, but instead I wash her plate, and Grampie's.

In my room, I switch to a green string.

I spend some time organizing my closet and scrubbing my bathroom. Mom will be happy when she sees that.

As I clean, I think. Mom said I was growing up too fast. But it's not a problem for me. I'm bigger than high school already. And I don't need art school later. Life is as good as art school. I just need to prove it to her.

I do homework until I hear Mom in the kitchen, and I go help her start the lasagna. Me cooking two meals in one day. Unprecedented.

It's a calm night. Grampie waits for his favorite meal

51

out in the garden. I can see him through the kitchen window, and I know he's humming, just like he always does when he's working. Mom hums a little, too.

While dinner's cooking, I sketch Grampie among the flowers.

And now it's Monday.

Getting ready this morning, I wanted to choose a purple string because I'm so excited about Palette, but I went with blue because it's only Monday. I have a whole week of school to get through before I start work.

I put on stacks of necklaces. White Doc boots. Black lipstick. Nick waits for me at school. Soon I'm sitting in Spanish class trying not to watch Jewel.

I'm not proud of my lingering crush. It's there, always there. Like my arms. Like the salt in the air of Ballard.

I've known him since elementary school, but mostly from a distance. One of my earliest memories: jumping in puddles with him at recess on a kindergarten day. It's strange how, in that memory, I can so clearly see little Jewel through my younger eyes, all huddled up in a white-and-black-striped snow hat and these red mittens he used to wear. I can't see anyone else; I don't even exactly remember what our kindergarten teacher looked like. But I've got this memory-film of Jewel, complete with the scent of rain and the shimmer of wet leaves. Maybe I'll paint that.

During middle school at Ocean Tides, I was busy with new friends, including Holly, while Jewel stayed at the public school. I guess that's when he got really close with Alice Davis.

When I started at Gates, I was so relieved to see that public middle school hadn't turned Jewel into a drone, like Mike Corrigan and those sports guys. Those guys who exist at every high school with a football team. They might grow out of the cretin stage, but probably won't. Destined to become frat boys. I'm pretty sure Mike or one of his buddies was behind the Sharpied "freak" on my desk freshman year.

All through Spanish class, I watch Jewel.

I watch him watch nothing. There's got to be a movie inside his brain.

Jewel stares a lot of the time.

I love that stare.

For a while in the fall, he let me behind it. He let me in.

I wondered sometimes if it was only because Alice was dating someone else, but I was able to push that idea aside because I was having so much fun with Jewel. I felt so close to him. I didn't want to think about Alice.

We painted together in my garage, and we kissed, and Grampie and Jewel talked about old movies. The feeling of Halloween was in the air. We talked and talked, and it seemed so real, so much like we were this couple who belonged together. He said yes when I asked him to the

Halloween Bloodbath. The dance where being a freak served me well and I was voted Halloween Queen.

Everything was natural during those days with Jewel. I didn't change my hair once. It only lasted a few weeks, though; he began to seem distracted, and then he was hanging out with Alice again and told me that he wasn't the right guy for me.

What he meant was that I'm not the right girl for him.

It's like he was just trying me out, and while I had the role for a while, he replaced me before the big opening night. Which is what, really?

Spring Semi, I guess. The big spring freshman and sophomore dance, the warm-up for junior and senior proms. If a sophomore couple starts out in the fall and makes it to Spring Semi, they'll probably make it all the way to graduation.

So that's the other reason I'm psyched for my job at Palette. If you can't get over your feelings for someone you can't have, maybe you should find someone else to fall for. Like an artist, or a new coworker. A blond guy on a skateboard. At least stay busy and forget how you love to watch Jewel watch nothing.

Finally it's time for Smith's art workshop, the only place where I feel free to relax at school.

We sit down on our stools—I try not to watch as Jewel sits with Alice, and Smith starts to psych us up for the spring art show. What should I enter? I have no idea.

"Push your limits," Smith says.

He reminds me of the teachers at Ocean Tides.

Mr. Smith doesn't follow some curriculum. The rest of my teachers drone through the day. He tries to inspire.

Whatever I put in the show needs to be awesome, because I won the fall art show.

"Browse my books for ideas," he says. "And the computer is yours."

I hung out with Jewel at the fall show, a rare time when Alice was nowhere around him, right when things were starting to happen between us. I'd made a city out of cardboard boxes that I found by the school Dumpster. Those boxes called to me. They begged to be buildings.

Right now, nothing's begging me to become anything.

"Here's your chance to show me what you've got," Mr. Smith says. "Show everybody what you're about."

I need to do something great.

Something that will make them know that I am ready for so much more than just a high school art show. That I'm the real deal. A real artist.

Jewel's messing around with a stack of photos, trying to put them in some kind of order. Alice is making a collage using what might be scraps from his discarded photos.

I am just sitting here. I'm trying to look deep in thought. Contemplating my masterpiece.

Mr. Smith comes over and taps the table, like knocking at a door. "Anyone home?"

"Yeah." I don't have to lie to him, though. He gets me. "But I'm stuck. I have no idea what I want to put in the show."

"Take off your boots."

I just do it. I step off my stool, bend down, and unzip my left Doc, then my right. "Am I gonna practice being grounded in my bare feet or something?"

He laughs. "How many times do I have to tell you, Vanessa, that I am not a hippie?"

"So what's with the shoes? How does this help me?"

"Paint them."

"My boots." He wants me to paint on my boots?

"Your boots. Still life."

"Paint a still life of my boots."

"Or draw them. Use any medium. I don't care. Just get your art muscles going." He picks up the boots and puts them on the table, brings me a sheet of paper. "Get flowing."

I nod. I fight the temptation to draw *on* my boots.

He goes off to check on someone else.

I start at the toe, trying to get the curve just right, starting in on the stitching that holds the leather to the sole.

I focus.

Once I have the whole bottom of the boot, the sole and the toe and the heel, I take a breath. Close my eyes. Open them. Look at my work.

It looks just like the boot. But it doesn't make me feel anything.

At least making it took me out of my head for a little while.

After workshop, it's time to come up with a plan to hook up Holly with her Wilson.

Got to find him first.

At lunch, I tell Nick, "We're on a hunt."

"Ooh, hidden treasure?" He eats a chicken finger.

"Holly's treasure."

He stands up and puts his hand above his eyes, peering out.

Then he sits. "Near the milk machines. Orange hoodie."

I stand quickly, take a peek. The Harry Potter glasses. The extrashort brown hair. "He's cute!"

"Duh."

"And he will look so very adorable with Holly."

"If he ever opens his eyes and notices her."

"That's what Holly has me for. Call me Cupid."

"Cupid."

I shoot an imaginary arrow at his heart with my invisible bow.

"Seriously, Vanessa, do we think it's wise to get involved in the love lives of innocent orchestra musicians?"

"Please. Holly has no idea how to talk to a guy by herself. You've seen her. She's smitten. She thinks Wilson's this genius. I'm sure it paralyzes her when she's around him."

"But if she could just chill out and talk to him, he'd love her. They have stuff in common."

"Exactly. So they just need a nudge."

"And you are the designated nudger."

"Precisely."

I spend the rest of lunch listening to Nick rehash some old movie and working out a plan in my head. Step one: recon on Wilson. Make sure he doesn't have a girlfriend. If he does, abort the mission. I am not a heartbreaker.

Six

Tuesday morning, as I'm riding my cruiser to school, I pass graffiti that stops me.

To call it graffiti seems wrong. It's blackbirds, in silhouette, against a gray concrete wall—the side of the Wash-O-Rama launderette.

Blackbirds. Simple. Beautiful. Appearing out of nowhere. Just landing. I know they must've been stenciled, to be so neat at the edges. But they feel so natural.

I did a series of birds a few months ago, in clay. They were tiny and I tried to make them perfect. But they never made me stop in my tracks the way these birds do.

I don't think I want to do birds again, but all of a sudden I'm pretty sure that spray paint is the right medium for me.

Does Palette sell it? On Saturday, I'll look.

In art workshop, while Jewel is out taking photos around the school and Alice is sketching something at their table, I use Smith's computer.

I search. *Public art.*

I read about the Guerrilla Girls, a group of women who make big statements about feminism by pointing out things like the percentage of women represented in New York's Metropolitan Museum of Art who are naked versus not naked. The Guerrilla Girls wear gorilla masks, and they make bumper stickers, billboards, and other paraphernalia. Cool, but not quite what I want to do.

I search for public art in Seattle and find out about a guy named Jason Sprinkle, who made big social statements all over town, doing things like tying a giant ball and chain around the leg of the *Hammering Man*, a huge metal statue outside our art museum. He also left a car blocking traffic right outside Westlake Center. I was just a kid, but I wonder if Mom remembers.

For me, there are two problems with that kind of art: One, you can get in a lot of trouble. Jason Sprinkle was arrested.

Two, you need a big statement to make.

I realize that I have no statement. I might look like I do, and I might be able to squeak out art projects that impress the high school world, but really. What is my statement? It can't just be that being different—being a freak, even—is okay. Too easy.

I can't stop thinking about those blackbirds. All I really want is a symbol that will make people feel something, the way those birds did to me.

So I search again. *Seattle. Graffiti. Spray paint. Tagging.*

Wow. I find lots of images. So much color. So big. How come I've never noticed this part of my city?

I feel myself speeding up, like I've found a way to go beyond high school and my same old life. A way to make other people stop and feel something. I sit very still because it's like my insides and my brain are moving too fast for my body to keep up. This is something new.

My boot still life comes back to mind, and I realize that the blackbirds are still too. But they are so much more than lines on paper. Those birds are absolutely free. They don't need to move to be moving.

Who cares about the spring art show when there's this?

Mr. Smith comes up behind me and says, "Stick around after class." *Good!* I'll get to be late for gym, and I'd rather hang out with him than with most people.

For about two seconds, I'm worried that he looked over my shoulder when I was on the computer and is about to lecture me about respecting property. He doesn't need to worry about that. I'm not planning to tag buildings. Just, I feel like I really want to use spray paint somehow.

But that's not what he wants to talk about.

He hands me this application. "Here—a job teaching art at the summer program at the elementary school. You'd be a great influence on these kids. And it's a paying gig. They're interviewing over spring break, and doing a few training sessions before school gets out."

"Well, thanks for thinking of me," I say, "but I already have a job. At Palette? The art shop?"

"Great place," he says. "That sounds like a good spot for you. But take the application anyway, just in case. Make an old teacher guy feel like he tried his best."

I take the paper and shove it into the bottom of my messenger bag as soon as I'm in the hallway.

The recon on Wilson is easy. Nick takes care of it during gym class on Wednesday. Apparently, locker-room talk is powerful stuff, and Nick gets lucky enough to hear Wilson defend the honor of some football player's girlfriend when said football player (not Mike Corrigan, but they're all the same) is bragging about his escapade.

Nick tells me at lunch that Wilson actually stepped in

and said, "Don't be a jackass." The guy, of course, mocked Wilson for being too much of a pussy to get any.

Then Wilson said, "If I had a girlfriend, I'd treat her with respect. Why is that so hard?" Nick says, "Wilson's too good to be true."

He's perfect for Holly. And her mom might actually approve of him.

I follow him to his locker after lunch.

After school on Wednesday, I get down to the second stage of Operation Wilson.

This is a special project, so it requires special materials.

I have an old wooden jewelry box; it's filled with my mom's unworn necklaces, earrings, pins, and rings. She has no use for them at the docks. Or on the couch.

The box has been in my room since I was born.

I dig out my beading and jewelry supply box.

I sit on my bed and find what I'm looking for. The little locket.

It's rose gold with swirly etchings.

No picture inside the locket. That's for Holly to do later.

The locket on its own is absolutely gorgeous but not quite sparkly enough.

I take it off its simple chain and set about making a new one. If I were doing this for myself, I'd choose deep pinks and oranges and blacks—colors of fire and shock. But for

Holly, I search through the beads and find the bag of tiny faceted crystals with the faintest purple tinge. Her end of the spectrum—pretty, but not showy. Perfect for one of her performances. I was going to make her a birthday necklace out of these beads last year but never got around to it. Perhaps fate wanted me to wait for Operation Wilson.

I cut a length of fishing wire and weave an intricate pattern. One bead after another, I make wishes for Holly. *For luck. For happiness. For beautiful music.* I imbue the necklace with good luck.

Later that night, Holly calls. "Are you still coming to the concert on Friday?"

"Absolutely. Looking forward to it. I know how much you've been practicing."

"Yeah. I have to. It's the best orchestra I play with. And I have a solo."

"I know, I know! You'll be brilliant."

"Back to work," she says.

I'm back to my own work, chewing the end of my purple pen.

Thursday morning, after Nick heads off to his homeroom, I turn toward Wilson's locker. Number 862. I'll be late for homeroom, but it's essential that no one see me.

I linger by the water fountain until everyone's gone. The late bell rings as I dig in my messenger bag for the letter.

I wrote it out by hand, very retro, wishing I had an inkpot and a quill. That's what Holly would want, if she were really writing letters to Wilson.

I made the envelope out of photos of outdoor scenes— all green grass and blue sky. First I collaged. Then I folded. The letter is written on plain white paper of a good stock, stuff I had for sketching. Nice. Very Holly.

I slide the note through the slots in locker number 862, my hands shaking just the tiniest bit, my heartbeat speeding up. It's like looking at art.

There's no way the Guerrilla Girls have this much fun fighting for women's rights.

I went for simplicity.

I've noticed you. I hope you've noticed me too. We'll soon find out.

Look for me.

I'll be wearing a gold locket, and smiling at you.

Mom, Grampie, and I order pizza on Thursday night.

Grampie asks, "What are you up to this weekend?"

"Going to Holly's concert on Friday, and then you know I'm starting my job on Saturday."

Grampie says, "I've got a poker game on Friday." His old buddies from the docks.

"No special plans for me," Mom says.

"Come to Holly's concert tomorrow. It's her big Seattle Youth Symphony Orchestra concert at Benaroya Hall. She has a solo! I'm sure she can get tickets for both of us."

Mom picks up her pizza slice. "That does sound special."

"Mother-daughter night," I say. "Let's do it." She smiles. I nod. "We'll need to leave by six-thirty."

"I'll be ready. Can't wait."

Neither can I. Operation Wilson will be in full swing.

Seven

I'm wearing a black T-shirt dress to the concert, simple makeup, pink fishnets, and my Doc boots. Nothing too wild, as I'll be with my mom and it's at the symphony hall. I don't want to freak out whatever spirits of classical musicians might be hanging around.

I decide to paint my nails silver.

Once my nails are dry, I toss a skinny-tipped Sharpie in my messenger bag so that I can decorate them later.

Mom and I take the bus because it's easier than parking downtown. We show up early so we can catch Holly before she goes to warm up. She needs to give us the tickets.

Mom's wearing her one and only skirt, which she bought for a wedding in 2006. It's black, and it pretty much just hangs on her, down to the middles of her knees. She's paired it with a white button-down shirt from the same era.

We're meeting Holly by the stage door of Benaroya Hall. As we walk from the bus stop, I pull the necklace from my messenger bag, unwrapped. "A gift for Holly."

"That's lovely," she says. I hand it to her for a closer look. "Is this my locket?"

"I didn't think you'd mind. It's not like you're using it. You never—" I almost say *You never wear anything pretty.* "You never dress up."

She closes her eyes for this long second, and says, "Next time, ask."

Mom hands the necklace back just as Holly and her parents walk up, Holly wheeling her cello. Holly's in perfect-fitting, elegant black trousers, a black tank, and a knit shrug. Hair twisted into a fishtail braid at the side. She looks just right for the stage. Mr. Warner is wearing a suit, and Mrs. Warner is in a tailored navy dress; next to her, my mom looks young and unsophisticated.

The Warners shake Mom's hand, say nice to see you again, while Holly props her cello against the door; then she and I hug. Everyone is watching as I hold up the necklace.

"I love it!" she says. "Thank you! The perfect good-luck charm."

You have no idea how lucky, I think as she fastens it on.

The concert is glorious. I don't actually know what's what when it comes to orchestral performances or classical music, but I can tell this is awesome. The music swells and quiets and travels around the concert hall. It strikes me that music is this thing you can't see at all but you can sense in your bones. It's absolutely there, even if it's just made of sound.

And somehow, when music gets in your bones, it makes you wonder about things. I tear up at one point, imagining what it would be like if Jewel were with me right now, sitting with me and my mom. I have to bite my lip to keep from crying because I'm wishing so hard. I can feel his absence to the left of me, where a stranger sits, maybe even more than I'd feel him if he were there.

At another crescendo, I think about Grampie and how he's been looking so much older. I feel his absence too, even though I'll see him later.

I snap out of it when Holly does her solo. The spotlight shines on her hair, her eyes are closed, her face is completely calm. Holly was born for this moment. Now I do cry.

I wipe my tears. She's such a star. Everyone in this giant hall is riveted.

Lucky Wilson. Soon he'll know she likes him. And then he'll know he can ask her out. It won't matter who wrote the letter once he realizes that Holly is meant for him.

Holly's mom and dad look so proud. As we all stand, clapping, I see Mrs. Warner wipe a tear from her cheek. Some music remains in my bones, and I can't help but wonder: What have I ever done to make my mom so proud?

Mom's clapping wildly, even letting out a wolf whistle.

There's a reception in the lobby under the Dale Chihuly chandelier; the one that looks like a wineglass.

The lobby is swarming, but I'm focused on one thing: Has Wilson seen the locket? Mom stands by my side as I crane my neck.

Holly shows up, and as I hug her, I look around.

I spot him standing by a table of miniature food and red punch, scarfing down tiny quiches. So, no. He hasn't spotted the locket. No one who was just made aware of a crush would be calmly eating quiches.

Mom and Holly's parents start to chat.

"I'm so thirsty." I grab Holly's arm to lead her to the punch.

It takes a little maneuvering, but I position Holly next to Wilson. He turns—my vision goes slow-motion with anticipation—and sees the locket where it hangs so gracefully around her neck.

Holly is oblivious to the locket's meaning, but I can tell she's trying to act natural in his vicinity. "I didn't think you liked fruit punch," she says to me.

I don't answer, because he's staring at her, his lips in an almost-smile. "It's you," he says.

"Uh," Holly responds. She's pretty much frozen.

Maybe I should've let her in on the plan. This would be less awkward. But she never would've gone through with it. She would've hidden in the background forever. It's better that she doesn't know why he's finally noticing her.

Wilson looks at me. "Hey, don't you go to Gates?"

"Yeah," I say. *Focus here, people. Focus.*

He turns to Holly. "Can we talk outside for a second?"

He's playing it so cool. He must be busting.

I nod at her: *Go*. They make their way through the crowd, and he guides her by the elbow. Good thing, because I doubt she could muster the motor skills to walk outside by herself at this moment.

I take some punch to my mom, who's now standing alone with a plate of little spring rolls.

Mom says, "Wasn't the concert wonderful?"

I'm really glad I invited her. We should do more stuff together, like we did when I was younger. "It was fantastic." I pop one of Mom's spring rolls in my mouth, watching Holly and Wilson through the tall window.

I take out the Sharpie and draw a little star on each of my pinkie nails. A tribute to Holly.

They come back through the door. They split, and he goes over to a balding man holding a violin case, who must be his dad. They head back out the huge door together.

Holly races over. She's glowing. Just like I knew she would be.

"Oh my gosh," she says.

"What?" Mom asks.

"Wilson asked me out!" She looks like she might take flight. I am so happy, I could fly myself.

"He's that cute guy she was just talking to," I tell Mom. "He goes to school with me. Nice guy."

Mom nods. "That's great."

"I'm so excited," Holly says.

I nod. She hasn't said anything about the locket. Did he mention it? "Awesome! So, what did he say?"

"He was glad to finally talk to me! He said he's noticed me and he thinks I'm really talented!"

"Smart guy." Mom reaches out and touches Holly's elbow.

"And he said he'd love to take me out for Thai food, or for burgers if I don't like spicy stuff! Or Indian if I'm vege-tarian! So sweet!" She grins. "How did I get so lucky?"

Hmm. Maybe he was embarrassed to mention the locket?

I have to tell her. If they go out and she doesn't know about the whole secret-admirer thing, it could get really awkward. She'll play it too low-key, for one thing. She needs to know that he knows she's into him and he's glad about it.

With people swirling around us, Mom biting down on a spring roll, I just let it out. "Actually, I sent Wilson a little anonymous note for you. Just a couple of lines, like a personal Cupid."

Holly turns her head to the side with the same look on her face that dogs get sometimes; the one that's straining hard to understand. Mom swallows.

"I stuck it into his locker. Nobody saw me. So he'd know someone had noticed him."

She squints.

"It said he should look for the locket tonight. To see who."

Her face sort of crumples, then turns pink. She reaches for the locket, cups it against her chest.

"Oh, Vanessa," Mom says. "You didn't."

"Look, it worked! It was helpful!" I *was* trying to help. And it *did* work.

Holly looks stunned. Blank.

"Right? Aren't you glad? He asked you out! He likes you back!"

"Glad?" she practically screams. "I've never been more embarrassed in my life!"

She grabs the necklace and yanks. Beads spill on the floor.

Holly stomps away.

I can't breathe. "Mom?"

She picks up the locket and starts walking toward the door. I follow. "I can't believe you'd be so inconsiderate of Holly. Your best friend."

"I only wanted to help. She'd never tell Wilson on her own."

"That's her business, Nessie."

"Well, but she wasn't doing anything about it! At all! She was just waiting around!"

"That's her business."

We walk out the front door toward the bus. Not talking. Mom keeps shaking her head, like there's been a tragedy.

The bus ride is silent.

I cannot stand it when my mom is upset and I'm the reason.

Mom goes to the kitchen. I go straight to my room.

I flop onto my bed.

I might explode.

I can't believe Holly's mad at me. I press my hands against my face.

I can't just lie there.

Mom's drinking tea at the kitchen table.

"Why are you so mad?"

She just looks at me.

"I was helping," I say. "I want Holly to have someone. I mean, don't you ever wish someone was there to sit next to you at things like that? Don't you ever feel this, like, absence?"

"Nessie, you were next to me. You're my someone."

Me? No. That's not what I'm talking about. "I'm your kid. That's different. You're still so young. You could have a life. And Holly can have something with Wilson."

"I'm more than okay with my life the way it is."

She's acting like that's the end of it, but I still feel the music in my bones, making me sad and making me long for something. Making me know that our little life is not enough. For either of us.

"For the record," I say, "I want someone next to me. Someone other than my family and my old friends. Someone who feels electric. And I think you deserve that too."

I walk back to my room, shaking inside.

Eight

Saturday morning, I wake up tired. I hardly slept, thinking about Holly.

Why was what I did so bad? I hate knowing that Holly has a reason to be mad at me.

I drag myself from bed and text her: "Great job. You rock." Better not to mention Wilson. But I've got to establish communication so that this gut-knot can unravel.

Mom's out, probably running errands; Grampie's in the garage. I toss on my longer black mini and a plain black tee, zip up my Doc boots, sling my messenger bag across my body, tie on a green string—very average—and hustle out the door to Palette for my first shift.

On my bicycle, I smell salt water, as usual. It's the sound, mingling with the fine mist of rain.

The cherry blossoms are close to popping.

I get to Palette ten minutes before ten o'clock, when I'm due, and find the door locked, so I lean against it. I look out between the low buildings across the street—the Mexican restaurant, the Secret Garden bookstore, the tattoo shop, the organic pet supply store—to where I can see a peek of the water. That water always makes me feel peaceful and safe, a response I inherited from Mom and Grampie, I guess.

I want to chew my nails, but that's why I've been keeping them painted: if I like how they look, I won't mess them up by biting them.

Instead, I twist the green string.

There's a beep and I look up to see Oscar honking from his orange Vespa, which he's parking.

As he takes off his checkerboard-pattern helmet, I wonder, how much would I have to save up for a scooter? It would be awesome to get around that way instead of pedaling and walking and busing. Turning sixteen was not a magic ticket to vehicular bliss. I will never be surprised with shiny keys. "You have to earn something like a car," Mom says. If I work through the summer, maybe I can manage a scooter.

Oscar throws me a peace sign as he walks over.

"Hi there." I stand up straighter, shuffle over to unblock the door.

"Hey, Vanessa," he says. Somehow, I'm a little surprised that he remembers my name.

He unlocks the dead bolt, we walk inside, and I feel this tingle. The whole world should be watching as I step into what might be a new life.

My first job. It's like the first day of school, only instead of counting down the days till it ends, I'm gearing up for a good time.

"Maye will be here soon to train you on the espresso machine," he says. It looks complicated, with lots of knobs.

"Great."

"Stash your stuff here," he says, walking around the main counter to a plywood shelf under the register, where I put my messenger bag.

"Why don't you just look around till Maye shows up? Get used to the inventory?"

I've been here a thousand times, but now he's my boss. "Sounds good."

"I'll be in the back office, checking in some new stock that we can put out if it's slow later. I'll bring out your paperwork in a bit."

He clunks off, and I wander down the wide aisles and touch the brushes: horsehair, synthetic. I take a mental inventory of every type of paper: watercolor, drawing, multi-use. And the colors. When I really pay attention to the colors everywhere—the paints, the pencils, the markers—it almost makes me queasy. With possibility. Shades of everything.

I find the spray paint in the back corner, locked in a case. There are all kinds of nozzles and caps and other accessories to go with the cans. Fat markers too. In lots of different colors. I cannot wait to figure all this out for the new project that's forming in my brain.

I wind up at the espresso stand. The top is a metal slab with legs screwed into brackets on the floor, and the front is an old red refrigerator door on its side; it's covered in superhero magnets and rock-show stickers and bumper stickers. My favorite reads, "What if the hokey-pokey really *is* what it's all about?"

I love this, the way property is kind of disrespected for the sake of decoration. Making a statement where some people might think it doesn't belong. That's art.

I step behind the counter and feel as if I'm doing something naughty. The register on top of the metal slab looks like something from an old-school mom-and-pop drugstore. I have no idea how to work it.

The shelves under the counter are filled with metal pitchers, recycled paper cups, plastic cups, lids, wooden stirrers, and canisters full of coffee beans, tea bags, and individually wrapped biscotti. Against the wall behind the counter, there's a sink, a milk-stocked fridge, an ice maker, two high-tech-looking drip coffeemakers, and an array of flavored syrups with pumps atop an old wooden dresser. The beautiful espresso machine is next to two hoppers filled with beans. One's labeled "Decaf only!" So I've learned that much.

I'm wiping down the counter, armed with a bottle of cleaner I found in the sink, when Oscar walks out of his back room. "Maye's here."

A girl is walking through the front door as she ties on a green Starbucks apron, obviously pilfered. She's tall with full arms and legs and a bit of a belly pooch, wearing a low-cut, raw-edged black T-shirt and bloodred A-line skirt.

Her look is so . . . bright.

A big turquoise rock dangles from a thick silver chain into her cleavage. Two tattoos—a bright green swallow and a yellow anchor—are visible at the edge of her shirt, where a lacy black bra also shows when she moves a certain way. Both arms are covered in classic tattoos: a bubble-heart, a rose, the word "Love" in a pretty script.

Maybe the best part is her hair: a heavy-looking mass of pure white dreadlocks. Platinum white. She looks like an angel descended from the planet Awesome.

This is exactly how I'd like to look. Modern pinup girl. With edge. And ink. Real ink, not just hair dye. Tattoos.

Maye: my new hero.

She walks over—it's almost like swimming, or yoga, the easy way she moves—and kisses Oscar near his ear. They're the same height, which is so adorable. "I'm Maye," she says, and stretches out her fingers toward me.

"Vanessa," I say. We shake. "At your service."

"I love your nails," she says.

"Likewise." Hers are done in a French manicure. Instead of white at the top, there's purple.

We kind of bow at each other.

She's so cool.

"Let me show you how this stuff works."

Oscar heads to the back room and Maye joins me behind the counter.

"Quick," she says, "what's the difference between a latte and a cappuccino?" I get distracted because that sunny blond guy comes in, his skateboard under his arm.

My hunch when I first saw him holds up: He seems like the slightly older version of Jewel. But where Jewel can be moody and cloud-hidden, James is the sun. Bright. Summer.

I can't resist thinking he might be exactly what I need to get over my mashed heart. I tear my gaze away and turn to Maye. "No idea."

"It's just the milk. Cappuccino is foamy. Half milk; half foam. That's a lotta foam. Latte is all milk with just a dab of foam."

"Easy enough. Cappuccino is extrafoamy. Got it."

"When in doubt, latte. Only the real connoisseurs like cappuccinos, and we don't get a lot of them in here." She pointedly shifts her gaze to James, who's propping his board against the funky couch. She raises her voice. "Right, James?"

He walks over. "Absolutely," he says. "And a mocha is just a latte with chocolate syrup. And lots of whipped creamy goodness. Might I get one of those right now?" He waggles his eyebrows at Maye.

"Indeed," Maye says. She reaches down for a metal pitcher. "James, this is the latest and greatest, Vanessa." She nods her white-dreaded head at me. "Vanessa, James. Skater-boy and photographer."

"Don't forget friend and lover," he says.

Lover.

"Maybe when you get the rare opportunity to woo some unsuspecting young rose, I suppose," Maye says. She pulls out the jug of whole milk.

"It's been a while." James hangs his head, as if he's ashamed.

"He's kind of heartbroken," Maye says as she pours milk into the pitcher.

I'm collecting facts like brushstrokes, building the portrait of this guy. Adorable. Youngish. Available. Possibly vulnerable. Definitely adorable.

"Who isn't heartbroken?" I say.

They both look at me as if I said something profound.

"I'm not, kid," Maye says. *Kid.*

"Oh, you and Oscar. So adorable it's disgusting. Gag me," James says. But he's smiling.

Oscar comes out of the back room carrying a box. He flashes a grin at us as he walks to a row of shelves and begins stocking watercolor palettes.

James squats and fiddles with the magnets stuck to the espresso counter, staging a battle between Batman and Superman. It's something Nick would do.

"So, even though most of our customers don't order anything too fancy, I take pride in this sweet puppy." Maye pats the machine. "I call her Betty."

"Then so will I."

I'm about at the top of my happiness. Purple string when I get home. I should've known. Should've brought it with me. This is exactly how I wanted my first day to go.

"So," she says. "The art of steaming milk."

The daily paper is lying on the counter. She plucks the rubber band from around it and uses that rubber band to gather the top snakes of dreads out of her face. Pebbles Flintstone meets Gwen Stefani.

"It's not difficult, but there is a knack to it. Skim foams the quickest, but it's lame. Airy. So I'll teach you on whole. You'll learn how to get the velvety stuff." She pours milk into the pitcher, takes me through the whole process.

I lean next to her to watch what's happening in the pitcher. Hear the hissing of the steam wand. I'm impressed by how much she seems to know, and how much she seems to care about it.

It feels almost indecent, standing this close to a person I just met. An espresso-machine diva.

"Keep the wand close to the surface of the milk," she says. "That's how you get foam. If you don't want foam, then just stick it in the middle and watch the temp. You're shooting for a hundred and forty degrees.

"You try," she says, and lightning-fast, I'm holding the pitcher. I pull the milk down too low and the wand sputters. She puts her hands over mine, nudges it back.

James stands up. "Who would win in a fight? Batman or Superman?"

Maye leans on the counter. "Pretty evenly matched. Superman has actual powers, but Batman has those wonderful toys."

The thermometer shows 130 degrees. The milk smells like hot marshmallows. I realize I need to turn the knob to turn off the steam, but I don't exactly have a free hand. "Um, how . . . ?"

Maye comes to my rescue, flips the handle on the steaming wand, and the wand quits steaming. "You'll get the hang of it," she says. "And you'll get strong wrist muscles, too."

"Thanks for the rescue," I say to her. Then I look straight at James and say, "Superman. I've always thought so. I mean, he wouldn't even have to fight. He could just fly really, really far away."

Maye finishes off James's drink, hands it to him without charging him. He says, "That's not winning. That's avoidance. I'm a Batman guy myself."

"But Batman can't escape to outer space." I could debate the superhero thing all day, and it seems like he could too. That makes me smile.

I take a step toward the sink, and my boot sticks. I bend down. Yep. Gum. "Eww," I say. I get a napkin to shield my fingers while I attempt to pull off the chewed Bazooka.

Maye's wearing saddle shoes. Perfect for the Palette espresso stand. I've gotta get a pair. Unofficial uniform.

In the immortal words of *Annie*, which Grampie still likes to watch with me around Christmastime even though it has nothing to do with Christmas, *I think I'm gonna like it here.*

Oscar shows me little details. The extra register tape is on the shelf by my bag. The key for the spray-paint case is in the main register's drawer. Business picks up and he teaches me how to work the register. I get the hang of it, but I'm slow because I can't stop checking out everything that customers buy and imagining what they'll do with it.

Most people are eager to talk about their projects. A woman tells me that she's doing a paint treatment on a crib that her husband built for their daughter's first baby, who will be born any day; an older man buys clay and tells me that he molds it to help with his arthritis; a girl about my age buys a sketchbook to bring to the museum.

During my lunch break, I buy a hot dog from the cart outside on the corner and eat it on a bench at the skate park, watching people almost fly around the giant concrete bowl, enjoying the no-drizzle, warming-up weather, and just liking the way it feels to be on a break from my job. Having a lunch break makes it feel official: I have a break from *something*. Something pretty great.

When I get back to Palette, there are a few customers but no one ready to be rung up, so I head to Maye, who's wiping down Betty. "I clean her constantly," she says. "Gotta keep her happy and shiny."

"That's a good way to be," I say. Happy and shiny. Yeah.

Oscar comes over. "Maye, you leave at three, right?"

"By then, yeah." She looks at me. "I've got a show going up at Ballard Art Collective. We're having a little opening party. I need to get over there early to set up."

Oscar turns to me. "We'll close the espresso machine early today. Use the out-of-order sign. Keep the drip coffee going, though." He walks off.

"So, are you psyched for your show?" I ask Maye.

"Oh, yeah," she says. "These dolls have been cluttering up my apartment for way too long. I need people to fall in love with them and *buy* them."

86

Wow. She's so blasé. I'd be freaking out with excitement, and probably nerves, too.

"Dolls?" I picture Victorian statuettes, with real-looking hair in curls and dresses like doilies.

"Yep. Rag dolls. Some fairies. Just creatures from my brain. I pretty much worship at the altar of Tim Burton, so some of my stuff looks like it'd fit right into *The Nightmare Before Christmas*."

"Cool." Might text Nick to go to Rain City and pick up that movie with me tonight, and hunker down.

She grins. "Want to see them?"

"Absolutely."

She goes around to the main register and comes back with her purse, red leather with oversized silver buckles, and pulls out a digital camera. We huddle together and she clicks through the images: dolls, but all so *her*. My favorite is dressed all in black and white stripes, like that cap Jewel had on for the kindergarten puddle-jumping that runs through my memory. The doll has metallic hair and her dress is poufy at the bottom, with a top like a corset. Her nose has a crystal on it, like it's pierced.

Honestly, though, I wonder if these dolls are such a big deal. They're mini-versions of Maye herself, and that's cool, but I do wonder if they're . . . art? I tell myself to quit judging. This girl is awesome.

"Your own show, that's so amazing." Now I sound like a

total fangirl. "All I've ever done is the school art show, whoop-de-do."

"Hey, you gotta start somewhere," Maye says. She's almost as optimistic and cheery as Holly. "The Collective is no big deal, actually. It's a small gallery. But definitely a step up from selling at the Sunday market, like I used to do. I'd sell two dolls, and then go blow the money on crepes. I couldn't sit at the market all day smelling those things and then not get one."

She pulls off the Starbucks apron, hangs it on the corner of Betty, and goes to the back room, reemerging moments later with Oscar.

"See you at nine," he says, pecking her cheek.

I stand behind the main register. "Later, Vanessa," she says, and does a little twirl on her way out the door.

I work at the register while Oscar stocks shelves and helps customers.

I could stay here all night, but too soon, it's time to close. Oscar's due at Maye's opening.

When they told me about it, was that an invitation to go along?

If Oscar just says good night, I'm not invited. If he lingers, I am.

"All-righty," he says, putting on his black denim jacket. "Schedule looks okay? Same time next Saturday?"

"Yep." I pick up my messenger bag.

"It's been great having you here. Have a good Satur-day night!"

Not invited.

"You too," I say. Going to Maye's show would definitely be more fun than going home. But I can work on some-thing of my own, or redo my nails, or color my hair. Call Nick about watching that Tim Burton movie. See how his Superhero Origins fest was last night.

Maybe I could call Holly. I still feel tied up inside over her being upset. If it weren't for that, I'd be at double-purple status.

I probably shouldn't call yet. She never texted me back.

I don't feel like going home. Standing outside Palette, I shut my eyes, smell the salt water, listen to a motorcycle go by.

I'll pedal to Golden Gardens, to the beach. There's time before dark.

The bike ride is like some other life; I'm drifting between eras. I've traveled this same path so many times, out of the shopping part of Ballard, past the rock-climbing gym, closer to the water. Up ahead, there's the marina, where boats live, majestic. The fish-and-chips shop with the huge soft-serve ice cream cones.

But now I ride this route as someone with a job. I picture a film in my head, showing me as a little girl, brown-haired, wearing a sweet dress that my mom found at Kidz Consign. Then the film switches to me during my Ocean Tides days, with my first bleached streaks and a string around my wrist, wearing jeans and a black tee. Then the film focuses in on me now, in brighter contrast, with my pink hair and my white boots.

I add on to the film: me, looking like Maye. Turned up a notch or ten, like a living doll.

I ride past the parking lot for the Ballard Locks, where fresh water from the ship canal mingles with salt water from Puget Sound. The canal and the sound are kept apart by huge gates on either side that reach all the way to the bottom. Boats traveling the canal have to stop between the two gates before being let out the other side. Inside the gates is the only place where the salt water and the fresh water mix.

Salmon run at the locks. The enormous schools of sock-eyes come in July, scales shimmering, returning to the place where they were born, now to spawn.

But what I love most at the locks isn't the boats or the salmon. Those are what Mom loves, for sure. For me, it's all about the flower garden on the grounds.

I remember being a kid on a summer day, wearing a

white dress. We passed through the garden on one of the walks Mom and I used to take. The roses were the prettiest things I'd ever seen. Looking back, I feel almost as if, in that moment, the roses could have become to me what water is to my mom. The thing that beats inside my chest. The thing that fills me up.

I plucked the top off one, right at the blossom, where there were no thorns.

Mom said, "Not for you!" It sounded harsh. She softened and said, "The flowers are here to feed the bees. We don't pick them."

It's one of my earliest memories: feeling guilty for killing a flower that belonged to the bees, and not to me.

I tried to reattach the flower to its bush. I petted the petals, stroked them, willed them to reattach.

My mom got teary. She bent down, arm on my back.

"The bees, Mommy," I said.

"They'll be all right," she said. "Look. More roses."

I looked. The garden was glorious. "More flowers," I said.

The air smelled of perfume not unlike Grampie's pipe smoke, but cleaner.

The Golden Gardens parking lot is scattered with cars. It's not what people in most cities would consider beach weather, but it's not raining and there's an edge of warmth in the air. In Seattle, that's enough to bring people out of their houses. Groups are having little fires as the sun sets, barbecuing, taking walks in bare feet.

I lock my bike to a bench and start toward the water.

In my boots, walking on the rocky beach is a challenge. I only get to the volleyball nets before I decide to sit on a huge piece of driftwood and stare at boats and people.

Being near the water seems like a good way to end my first day at Palette.

I wish Nick and Holly were here too.

Nine

I text Holly three times on Sunday and call once. No response.

I think about taking the bus over to her house, but it's pretty obvious she doesn't want to see me. I don't know if she's still going to go out with Wilson. I don't know if I should find him at school and apologize. I don't even know if he knows I'm the one who wrote the note. All this not knowing makes me feel restless.

I finish my homework before lunch and decide to take my bike for a cruise.

I throw my jeans on under my splattered tank dress and

zip up my boots. Once I'm on my bike, I consider pedaling to Nick's.

No. There's somewhere else I want to go. I start pedaling.

I'm off to the gallery, Ballard Art Collective. It's closed on Sundays, but I want to peek in at Maye's work.

I roll up onto the sidewalk and sit there, looking in.

Maye's dolls are meticulously made. Each one of them has its own personality. They're bigger than I expected, each about three feet tall.

It's like they're alive. Some are sad and some are delighted and at least one is in love.

Still, I wonder. If I didn't know Maye, and I was just passing by, would I be impressed by what I'm seeing through the window? Would the dolls make me think? Make me feel?

In a way, they're not much different from a still life. They represent different moods, and they're well made, but are they really art? Do they have layers? In a way, it's kind of like they're the same thing as my strings, only on a larger scale.

Part of me wishes they could talk or something. After spending time learning about the Guerrilla Girls and Jason Sprinkle, I'm beginning to see that messages matter.

What's Maye saying with these dolls?

I sit still on my cruiser, feet to the sidewalk, just looking.

When I get home, I check my phone again.

No messages.

* * *

Monday comes too fast, as always, but this week I don't mind. The faster Monday, Tuesday, Wednesday, Thursday, and Friday pass, the sooner I get to go back to Palette.

I wake up with this weird feeling because I still haven't heard from Holly. I want to tell her about Palette. It was killer waiting around all day Sunday to hear from her.

I miss her. So much.

I tie on a yellow string and pedal off through the mist.

When I meet up with Nick outside of school, the first thing he says is, "Holly told me about the note."

When did they even have this conversation? I don't think they've ever hung out before, or talked, or anything, without me.

It's so none of his business. I hope I look . . . tough. Annoyed. "And?"

"And what were you thinking? You went way too far!" Outraged. As if I haven't already heard this from Holly. And Mom. And in the back of my own head.

"You know as well as I do that she wasn't going to do anything on her own. She was wasting time."

"If she didn't do anything, she would've had her reasons."

"You knew about the plan! You're the one who helped me figure out who Wilson even is!"

"I thought you were planning something low-key, like

running into him somewhere. Something natural. But this? A declaration of her feelings? Without even talking to her about it? Maybe she wasn't ready."

"It wasn't a declaration! It was subtle!"

But she *should* be ready. She's great; can't she see that? I can. Nick can. Now Wilson can too.

I get to class early, plop into my seat, and think.

People need to open their eyes and look at themselves. If Holly were confident, she'd have Wilson *and* she wouldn't be mad at me. If Nick could get over being different or whatever, he wouldn't be waiting for college to find a boyfriend. If Mom would stop seeing herself as old before her time, she could have a life. Grampie's pretty much the only person I know who does mostly what he likes, when he likes. And he looks like he might be forced to slow down soon.

Me? I need to go after James. He's like sunshine to me for a reason: I don't know him, but I sense that we're perfect for each other. It doesn't matter that I'm a little younger. I'm ready for him. I'm ready for anything.

Ten

I'm not even sure if Nick will show up for lunch, but then he sits with me at our usual table, and says, "About Holly. I understand you didn't think you were doing anything wrong." I can tell he still thinks it was wrong, though. "Man, I hate to see you with that yellow string. Are you okay?"

"I will be." *Let it go.* I don't need two friends mad at me.

"Holly will forgive you." He pops open his soda. "If you apologize."

Maybe I should. Just get past it. But that would mean admitting I was wrong, when I think good things will probably come. Wilson did ask her out. "We'll be fine," I say.

"I know," he says. "You guys have been friends for a long time."

I really do not want to talk about Holly with Nick. He and I are already dangerously close to another argument. "So," I say, biting my apple. "Someone put up a poster at Palette on Saturday. In the window, you know? Pride Parade is coming up."

"Yeah," he says. "I saw that in the *Weekly*."

"Let's go." I don't know if he's ever been to a Pride event, but it's the perfect opportunity.

I can't read his face. But he nods. "Could be fun."

Grampie's in a great mood this week, happy that he can get outside and garden. It may not seem like your usual hobby for a career longshoreman, but Grampie loves working with the earth almost as much as he loved working near the water.

The weather is glorious. Not too hot, but the sun comes out almost every day, for hours at a time. If Holly weren't locking me out, I'd invite her to hang out at Golden Gardens.

Jewel and Alice hold hands as they leave school, walking home together every day. I try not to watch. I think of James, and how he and I could make the perfect couple.

The longer I don't hear from Holly, the more school feels like a prison. So much of my real life is *out there*. But I'm stuck behind a desk, in a shuffle, at my table in the cafeteria.

By Wednesday, I can't handle being away from Palette any longer. I've had only one shift, and I've already started to think of it as the only place where I can actually breathe. It's even better than art workshop.

When I get there, Maye is in her Starbucks apron behind the coffee bar.

James—hallelujah—is standing at the counter, his board propped up on the stand.

Oscar's reading a magazine at the main register.

I can feel my cobwebs shaking away.

"Hey, Vanessa," Oscar says.

"Chica!" Maye says.

"Hey," I say.

"Anything up?" Oscar asks. "You're not scheduled today."

"Just felt like getting out of the house. Grab a hot chocolate. How are you guys?"

"Sick," Maye says, rubbing her belly. "I partied a little hearty last night."

Oscar sticks his finger in his mouth and makes a puking motion.

"Beautiful," I say.

James stirs packet after packet of sugar into his mug. "Hey, you gotta live."

Maye starts steaming milk for my chocolate. "You like a little coffee with your sugar, James?"

He gives me a smile that could melt icebergs. "Sugar is one of the finer things in life," he says. "Nice to see you again."

Why is my heart pounding like this? He's just a guy.

"You too." I pretend that it's just a conversation.

"So, Miss Maye, we're still on for later, right?" James asks.

"You mean Miss December," Maye says, and does a sexy little move with her shoulder, batting her eyelashes. "Yeah, we are."

James turns to me. "I'm producing a calendar."

"Pinup girls," Maye says.

"And she's the star."

Maye strikes a pose with her mouth all puckered, like Betty Boop. Then she rubs her temples as if she has the world's worst headache.

"Cool," I say. And a little raunchy. But what's wrong with that? She said pinup girls, not nudes.

"I've got setting up to do. Fuzzy dice to buy. A big-time trip to Archie McPhee," James says. He means the crazy party supply/kitsch store down the road.

James chugs his coffee as if it's a beer. And he's off, on his skateboard, through the store and out the door.

I wish . . . Yow. *Get a grip.*

"So your show opening was fun?" I ask Maye.

"So much fun!" she says. "Everyone was really into it."

"Congratulations." I straighten the napkins. "I was passing by on Sunday, and I looked in. Your dolls are amazing."

"Thanks!"

"They look alive. That's what I like about them. They seem as if they could wander around on their own." It's true. But I'm still wondering—does that make them art?

"I'm pretty sure they do, when I'm not looking," she says, chuckling. "Seriously, thanks. I spend so much time and energy on those dolls, it means a lot when people take the time to look at them."

"I loved seeing them." Also true.

"So, what are you working on, artwise?"

"I need to get something ready for the next school show, but I'm kind of blocked."

"Oh, yeah?" She's wiping down Betty, slowly.

"Yeah. I want to do something sort of guerrilla-ish. Some street art or something."

"Remember, it's all about the statement. What would you like to say?"

That's exactly what I'm not so sure of. "I'll get back to you on that. Um, you look kind of green."

"Totally and completely," she says. "Kermit green."

"Look, I'm here anyway. It's slow. Maybe you should take a rest. I can cover."

"Oh, would you really? Oscar's lounger in the back has been calling my name."

I grin at her. "Abso-snootly." Whoops. Kid talk.

She grins back. "You're the best."

She plops Betty's towel into the sink and disappears into the back room.

James comes back to pick up Maye for their photo session just before closing time. Oscar is counting down the big register drawer, Maye is hanging out on the couch, looking much better, and I'm scrubbing the coffee table in front of the couch.

I feel the whole world perk up when he glides in.

Maye stands up, grabs her purse. "Just need to stop home to change," she says. "And redo makeup."

"This gonna take all night?" Oscar asks.

"Should be fairly quick once the starlet is ready for her close-up," James says.

"Meet you at the Tin Hat after, then," Oscar says. He goes to put the money in the safe for the night.

James turns to me. "Will you be giving us the pleasure of your company at the Tin Hat?"

No one's actually invited me. And I'm five years shy of

being old enough to get into a bar. Then again, I don't think he's twenty-one either.

"Alas," Maye says, "Vanessa is a young'un."

"Obviously," he says. What does he mean by that? Just how young do I look?

"But then again, so are you," Maye says.

"My point exactly," James says.

"How old are you?" I ask, bold.

"My ID says I'm twenty-two," he says with a grin.

"Nineteen," Maye says. "Barely."

He pulls something out of his pocket and hands it to me. A license with his photo and the name Michael Smith.

"Gotcha," I say.

Maye takes off her apron and goes to the back room. Me and James. Alone.

"Too bad you don't have an ID," James says. "We could've had fun."

I have never before wished to grow up so fast. To have fun with a boy who is . . . what? *Sexy.* He's a man, and that means he's not just adorable or cute or even hot. He's sexy.

Awesome. And a little scary. But I can still have fun with him. Maybe even cross that line that Jewel and I got so close to. And if we go there, I'll make sure we use protection. This can happen.

"Yeah, too bad." But I can't give up this easily. "I mean, maybe we can have fun. All I need is an ID, right?"

He absolutely grins. "And I'm just the person to supply it."

I could get a tattoo if I had an ID. This is sounding better and better. "I don't have the right kind of picture."

"Good thing I have a camera," he says. "I've got everything we need, actually."

I smile. "Good thing."

"Yeah, it's kind of a side business for me."

A *side business?* In identity falsification? That's not so cool. It's actually kind of criminal. But you gotta live, like he said. And he doesn't seem like an actual criminal. Plus, he just said *we*.

"I work open-to-close on Saturday."

"Okay. I'll be here for you at closing time on Saturday."

That was so easy. "Sounds like a plan."

A plan to be alone with James. *All right.*

Oscar comes out from the back. "Time to go!"

I toss the rag in the sink and grab my bag from behind the counter.

"Glad you showed up today," Oscar says. "Big help."

"You're an angel," Maye says.

They head to the door, but James lags behind. Waiting for me?

"You have a fun night," he says.

"Thanks." I'll be . . . finishing my Spanish homework. That brings me back to earth.

Then we're all out the door. They're heading left and I have no choice but to turn right and go home.

I feel like they forget about me as soon as I turn the corner.

But it's okay. Something has changed.

I'll have my ID and I'll get to go wherever they go.

Eleven

All Thursday, I'm thinking about Saturday night. James. My official ticket into the real world.

I need to look older for the ID photo, so I'll shoot for sexy. I'll be irresistible, and he'll want me.

This is going to be so much fun.

Plus, spring break is coming up. Spring Semi, too, but I've barely thought about that.

Nick is being normal, thank the Goddess. I lay off the Pride thing, though. I planted the seed; now I'm giving it time so that I can be sure he really wants to go. I don't want to push him into anything, like I did with Holly. I still haven't heard from her.

Mr. Smith asks me again about applying for that summer teaching job. He talks me into getting an interview set up over spring break.

At lunch, Nick and I make plans to go shopping downtown on Sunday. Neither of us mentions Holly.

I'm starting to itch inside. I'm still thinking about the graffiti birds and Maye's dolls. Thursday night, I decide to go shopping for spray paint.

As I pick out a rainbow of six colors, a pack of caps for different effects, and a giant marker, I can barely keep my excitement inside. New toys!

At home, Mom and Grampie grab me to play Monopoly, so I hide my new supplies in my closet.

Finally, Saturday.

I wear my shortest black skirt, the pink fishnets, the black tee with metallic stars that Nick likes to borrow, and my white boots. All of my favorite things.

Somehow, I'm getting used to living with the idea that Holly's not exactly my friend right now. It's become this constant buzz that I can choose not to hear or feel because there are louder noises going on.

Blue string.

Extra time with makeup, repaint nails bright plum.

Maye keeps giving me these looks all day. I'm not sure why, but I'm trying not to think about it, add it to that buzz. I can't worry about Maye or Holly. Only Mission James.

Maye leaves early because we're slow, and it's the first time I've been relieved to see her go. I figure it's about the ID, but, I mean, if she's okay with James having one and making them, why would it bother her that I want one? She probably had a fake ID when she was my age. She's only twenty-two.

As promised, James turns up at closing time, minus his skateboard.

Oscar's busy counting down the register. I yell, "Good night!" and he barely looks up as he yells, "See ya!"

I walk over to James, feeling like I'm on a runway. He definitely likes my look.

He has the dirtiest hands, covered in black . . . grease? It's not paint. Not ink.

"I apologize for my raggedy appearance in front of a lady as lovely as yourself," he says, smiling. "I was working in the garage. Greasy."

"You're a mechanic?"

"I work on Vespas," he says. "When I'm not doing one of my photo projects."

I want a Vespa even more now. "That's awesome."

"Yeah, I fell in love with them a while back."

"So why don't you ride one?"

We start walking, me following his lead. "I do. I skate

around Ballard usually because I live here. When I'm going other places, I scoot when the weather's okay, and drive when it's not."

"Gotcha," I say. It hits me then that he probably has an apartment, alone. I'm hanging out—on a date?—with someone old enough to live by himself. Before, I'd pictured him somewhere filled with skateboards and cameras and sunshine and fun, but nowhere specific.

"Do you have roommates?" Wait. What if he still lives at home? Like, with his parents? I don't want to embarrass him. "I mean, who do you live with?"

"Just me," he says. "I grew up in Sammamish, but migrated to Seattle as soon as possible. I left high school during my junior year. Got my GED a year later. I just couldn't handle it anymore."

Handle what? "School?"

"School. Home. Everything. I'm much happier out here, doing my thing."

Exactly what I've been wishing for. A life full of whatever colors I feel like putting in. No boundaries. "Cool. GED."

He's so tall, and his long legs make his strides three times the length of mine. I try not to lose my breath as I keep up. "Wish I had my board with me," he says. "I feel naked without it."

We're out alone together and he's talking about being naked.

"I'd like to learn," I say. Then, for good measure, I throw in, "I was down at the skate bowl on my break the other day watching some guys glide around." *Glide around? That is so not official skater lingo.*

He doesn't seem to notice how lame I am.

"So, here we are," he says as we turn onto a little side street close to the canal.

"Um, where, exactly?"

"My place. Vespa shop boss gives me a great rent. Above the garage." He points, and I see that we are outside a Vespa garage that I'd never even noticed before. Probably because I'm not in the habit of ducking down alleyways.

"Oh," I say. We're hanging out here, at his place? *That's a whole other can of worms,* as Grampie would say. I hadn't really considered where we'd be going to do this ID thing.

He grins. "Follow me."

Anywhere.

My house is only about ten blocks from here. Yet I feel like I've crossed some invisible line. It's like the comic book of me has a whole new panel, all freshly penciled. Yet to be inked or colored.

I'm about to be a girl with a fake ID. The whole world is open to me. At last!

I'm grinning now.

James notices. "You have a cute smile."

"Thanks." I grin wider.

"But don't smile like that in the photo. No one's excited to be at the DMV, which is where you're pretending to be."

He starts walking up the rickety metal stairs to his apartment.

As I follow him up, I feel my new life coming over me. I imagine myself walking into a whole new thing, like if I shut my eyes I might open them and see everything through the eyes of a Cubist, or an Impressionist, or Jackson Pollock himself.

On these slippery steps, in my boots, I realize I'm also a little bit scared of falling.

He unlocks the door.

His skateboard leans up against the wall opposite the door, under a poster advertising the original Lollapalooza concert, in 1991. I wasn't born yet, and he would've been a little kid then. The whole apartment is one room, plus a bathroom, where towels and clothes are strewn. His bed is a mattress on the floor with the sheets half ripped off, and his couch is the cheapie one from IKEA that Mom said I could get for my garage studio if I wanted, but I opted for an open wall; more space to paint.

The kitchen is a tiny area next to the front door, with a mini-fridge and a microwave but no oven or stove. Plastic cups and paper dishes and bowls sit on the little chopping block that serves as a counter, with a rack for kitchen tools underneath that's filled instead with canned soup.

The place is kind of . . . depressing. Then again, he's only nineteen, technically a high school dropout. He makes half a living at the Vespa shop, probably, and the other half in fake IDs and calendars?

The walls are all white, except for a sky-blue square about four feet by four feet. James points at its center and says, "Painted to exactly replicate the background at the DMV."

"Smart." Wow. This really is a business for him.

"Gotta wash up," he says, wiggling his greasy fingers at me. "I'll be out in a sec." He shuts the bathroom door, and I hear the water running.

I look at his folding card table, where he's got a laptop, photo printer, scanner, and his digital camera plugged into a charger. It's an oasis of technology.

He walks up behind me. "Ready?"

I've never taken a driver's license picture. I'm sixteen, but I'll be a bus rider and bike pedaler till I can afford a vehicle.

"Of course I'm ready."

"Your shirt will show up nicely," he says. "Black's the best for head shots."

Head shot or mug shot? I've never done anything illegal before.

Chill out. This isn't a big deal.

He takes me by the hand and leads me into position in front of the blue square. His hand is still clammy from washing, but touching it makes me feel electrical sparks.

He holds my shoulders to position me. "Don't smile too big."

But if this is a mug shot, then I am the most smiley criminal ever.

He snaps photos. "Straight ahead. Try to look normal," he says when I can't quit grinning.

Whatever normal is. That only makes me smile more, because my sense of normalcy is changing so quickly, and I love it. So what if his place is dingy? It's *his*.

I need to get this ID photo done, so that we can start hanging out for real. Like how I used to with Jewel, only James is so much more ready for me. We can go anywhere together, and anything can happen.

I breathe deeply to calm down, and manage a few subdued shots.

Then, I stick my tongue out at him. I know we already got the shot, so I want to have fun. Pucker my lips. Do a Betty Boop face, like Maye.

He plays along, snapping photos of all my different poses, laughing.

I really get into it. I even do the classic hunched-shoulders couture pose.

Eventually, he goes over to his table and plugs the camera into his computer. "I think we got something there in the middle."

I sit on the couch, which puts the whole apartment between us. I can't help but glance at his unmade bed, imagine us lying there, all entwined.

He works silently, clicking away.

I wish he would put on some music or something. I'm staring at the wall, and I don't want to interrupt him. Maybe I should just pull off my clothes and get on the bed. Ha!

Can I do something? Should I do something? Does he want me to do something? My face is hot.

Am I crazy? I've been waiting for this moment all week. And I'm frozen.

After a few minutes, he's done. The printer whirs, and there it is, my very own false identity.

"Just have to take it into the copy shop to get laminated by my buddy there," he says.

This seems way too easy. What about the holograms the DMV uses? Still, he definitely gets into bars with his ID. "Thanks," I say.

What do I owe you? Is that what I should say? Or something sassy? *Let me repay you with a kiss?*

"Mission accomplished," he says. Something I would say too.

I nod. I don't want to leave, but there was something final in his tone. "Job well done." I stand.

Maybe he'll offer to walk me home, or give me a ride on his Vespa.

I follow him to the door, willing him to make a move.

114

It gets awkward on top of those fire-escape steps.

"See ya," I say, and open the door, thinking, Stop me. Grab me.

When he doesn't, I feel like crumbling.

As I go down the steps, I have one thing to hold on to.

He'll have to give me the ID and I still have to pay him. I'll be seeing him soon. And I will *not* freeze again.

My phone buzzes as I'm cruising home, Nick calling to make a plan for shopping tomorrow. Back in my room, I take out my phone.

It was Holly.

My insides seize up. Relief? Shock?

That's dumb. Stupid. Of course we'll get past this. I knew we would.

I don't even sit down. I just call.

"Hey."

"You called."

"I know. I have news. Something sort of happened, and it feels too weird to not tell you. I'm still not happy about the whole note thing, but . . . it does feel weird to not call you when I had the best date ever."

I gasp. I actually gasp. "Wilson? Holly! That's great!"

"I know!" All the tension is gone from her voice. "It was so wonderful! Nessie, I like him so much, and he says he likes me, too."

"So you guys went out."

"Mmm-hmmm. Tonight. He came by and met my parents and everything. They remembered him from the concert, from his solo. He knows they're kind of protective, so he picked me up at six and we just went to dinner."

"I'm dying here! This is awesome!" Oh my Goddess. It feels so good to talk to Holly. I feel off the hook. Life can get back to normal, only better.

"I know. I'm so, so happy about this. We just have so much in common!"

"So . . ."

"He kissed me in his car, when he dropped me off. It was the sweetest thing."

"I'm so happy for you!"

Then, silence. It's as if we've said all the happy stuff there is to say. I'm not off the hook.

"So, did you tell him about . . ."

"He doesn't know anything. He still thinks I wrote that note and had you drop it off for me."

"What does he think about it?"

"I guess he thinks it was brave. He said that. But it's the only part of this that makes me feel weird. It's not something I would do. You know that. I'm not actually brave with telling people how I feel."

"So you think he thinks you're someone you're not?"

"Kind of."

"But that's just a detail. He just spent a whole night

116

with you, and he kissed you and he obviously thinks you're awesome. He knows who you really are."

"I hope so."

"I know so."

We're out of words again.

"Holly?"

"Yeah?"

"Do you want to come shopping with me and Nick tomorrow? Westlake?"

She's quiet. I can practically hear her thinking. "Okay."

"Great. I'll text you details in the morning."

We hang up.

It's the best I've slept in days.

Twelve

On Sunday morning, Grampie and Mom are in the yard pulling weeds, and I know they'll be busy for a while. So I get out my spray paint.

I take the bagful of supplies into the garage and lay out newspaper from the recycling bin.

I choose the purple can first, with the super-fat nozzle.

I spray right onto the paper. It's like the can is part of my body. I love the feel of this brilliant color materializing as I squeeze. It's as simple, and as natural, as blinking. Breathing.

I'm not getting a lot of mist, just a wide line that I find

I can control easily. I even love the hiss. The purple is deep and glossy, wet-looking.

I just make squiggles. But there's so much movement in them, like electricity. I have to add orange right away.

This color has no bounds. There was no need to pencil first, or ink. Or even think. Just press and—kabam!—art.

Nick calls while I'm crumpling the paper. It kind of breaks my heart to get rid of it, but I'm not ready for anyone to see my new thing yet. This was a practice session to get the feel. I toss the paper into the garbage can as I click the phone to answer.

"We're going to Westlake, right? Please say you can still go, because my skin has totally freaked out. What do I do?"

"You wait for it to go away," I say. "To shrink, then be gone."

"That's poetically beautiful and all, but I need concealer."

"You know this pale girl has nothing for your olive tone."

"Duh," he says. "Your Barely There would look barely human on me. We'll pick something out at Westlake."

"Sure," I say. "Bus stop in fifteen. Hey. Holly's coming!"

"Yay! You two made up?"

"I think so. We'll see."

"That's great."

We hang up and I text Holly to say I'll tell her when we're on the 28 so that she can grab the same one when it rides through Fremont. She answers right away: "See you soon." I love that Holly doesn't use text-speak.

I get ready fast. Minimalist look today—my one and only pair of jeans and a plain black tee. Blue string.

If not for the pink hair, I'd look like every other girl downtown. The color is starting to fade a bit, though.

I rush into my boots and go out to the living room, where Grampie and Mom are watching an old movie.

"Heading to Westlake," I say.

Mom looks up. "Your homework done?"

"Yep."

"Then have fun."

I don't tell Mom that Holly's going shopping. I might jinx it.

At the bus stop, Nick is standing there in his casual way. "I'm so jealous of your perfect skin."

I have to look for his pimple; it's near his ear. "Nick, that zit is camouflaged by your hair."

"It so isn't. This zit has taken over." He covers his face with his hands.

No use arguing. "Yeah, you're hideous."

The bus shows up, and we climb on. I text Holly.

Nick asks about Palette, but I'm not sure how to explain it to him, the way I feel more alive there, and the way I've realized, once and for all, that I am so over high school, and quite possibly even over Jewel.

"It's fun. Once I get paid, you have to help me pick out summer clothes."

Then we're in Fremont, Holly's climbing onto the bus, and she's as full of light as ever. I'm so relieved to see her, I stand up, decide to make a moment of her. I skip down the aisle and give her the biggest hug.

She returns it.

We go back to Nick, and he hugs her too.

She tells him about Wilson.

"I think I just had a brilliant idea," Nick says. "Spring Semi! Wilson will ask you! We can all go!"

She grins. "A dance?"

"Nick, tell her. It's a big dance. Not my scene, really, but . . ."

"Yeah, Vanessa was Halloween Queen because that dance is all about the costumes and hers ruled. Spring Semi is more classic. It's your chance to be a princess, Holly. You'll go with your Prince Charming!"

Holly looks so happy. "If he asks me." She gives me a look. So does Nick.

"Dudes. Don't worry. I am not going to interfere. Have you heard from him?"

She blushes. "Text this morning."

We smile at each other.

"Hey, Vanessa."

"Yes, Nicolai, dear?"

"Will you be my date to the dance?"

I stick my tongue out at him, then grin. An hour ago, I wouldn't have thought the idea of a sophomore semiformal would excite me. But now it does. Holly's beaming. Nick's excited. "Abso-snootly!"

The bus stops and we hop off.

Inside the department store, air is recycled. They're pumping faux-classical versions of hard rock songs. Guns N' Roses by synthesizer. I feel something shift in me as soon as we walk in.

Holly's distracted by the dress section.

Nick's lagging. "Let's help Holly find a dress."

"He hasn't even asked me yet!" She's touching a sequined halter dress. "I'm not trying on dresses until he asks me! Unless he asks me."

"Then let's go pick out Vanessa's paycheck clothes."

"Nick and I have a mission." I want to get the makeup so that he can stop angsting over his zit and we can get out of here.

"I'm actually not so sure about the whole Dazzle thing. It might be weird." Nick can be like this.

"It's not weird. If you want concealer, you have every right to buy it. Right, Holly?"

She nods. "Sure."

"You wear guyliner, Nick. How is this any different?" I take his hand.

He walks with me. "I guess it's not."

I can see how it feels like a big deal, though. No other guy I know—not even James, who is more of a man than just a guy—would buy concealer at a makeup counter. Or anywhere. But maybe this is just part of Nick accepting himself. He *wants* the stuff.

The lady is ringing up a woman who looks about Grampie's age. The thought crosses my mind that Grampie wouldn't look so gray if he'd use some blush or bronzer, but that's silly. He wouldn't be himself if he did that.

Holly goes off to smell the perfumes while Nick kneels down to look at the display.

The lady ignores us, messing around with the credit card tape.

I pick up a sample tube of Pomegranate Juice Sleek Shine gloss. Squeeze it, dab a bit on my finger, and coat my lips.

Nick stands up. "That's hot."

I look in the mirror and have to agree. I pucker up. "Yeah. Like I'd pay fourteen dollars for this tiny tube."

The lady comes over, finally. "Can I ring that up for you?" she asks me, a smile revealing too-white teeth.

I shake my head and put the sample tube back. "Not today." I elbow Nick.

He says nothing.

I'm going to have to take the lead. "My friend here needs some concealer."

The woman looks at Holly.

"Not that friend. This friend."

The woman looks at Nick. She's still smiling, but her teeth aren't showing. Something's going on beneath her surface.

"What shade do you recommend?" I ask her.

"For him?"

Nick's pretending to study the lip glosses.

"She needs to see your face," I say to him.

She hesitates a beat too long before saying, "Let me grab my sample bottles."

She's not even talking directly to him! I need to fix the tension between Nick and me, and get him to see that he can be whoever he is and that no one will judge, but now this lady is being difficult. "He's just one of the girls," I say.

I feel Nick stiffen.

I crossed a line. A major line.

She moves her gaze over to me. "One moment."

She bends down to reach for a cover-up bottle.

And it's undeniable.

This lady rolls her eyes.

While she's searching for a color, Nick grabs my hand and leads me away. Holly follows.

"Grecian Beauty?" the woman asks as we walk off.

We walk past hosiery, past sunglasses, past handbags, and we're on the street.

People rush by.

Nick looks at me, wide-eyed, and I can tell he's expecting me to say something. I know. I know. I know. I've so let him down.

"Maybe you should just get something at the drugstore," I say. Lame.

He walks off toward the bus stop, Holly and I follow, and we ride home silently, him looking out the window, me biting my pinkie nail. Holly gets another text from Wilson, so she's distracted. "He wants to meet up." She's still beaming, but it's not quite the moment it was before.

When the bus stops in Fremont and Holly stands up to go, Nick says, "We're really going shopping once the dance is official."

"Definitely," she says.

I wonder if I'm still included in that scenario. I give her a weak wave, and she returns it with one of her own.

When we get off the bus in Ballard, Nick mumbles something about homework and heads toward his house.

I wander over to the skate park to sit.

From my bench, I watch the skater-guys doing tricks. One catches my eye. He wears a wool beanie even though it's getting warm out. He's got on long shorts, skate shoes, and a beat-up T-shirt. It crosses my mind that he should have pads, a helmet.

The guy is so into what he's doing. He's working in the big concrete bowl, gliding from one side to the other. He must have so much focus, to be able to just do that. He's totally in this moment. His board is part of his body.

As he approaches the lip of the bowl, I see a shift in his body right before he tries to do a three-sixty turn. He doesn't quite catch the board right as he lands. Sliding down to the bottom of the bowl must burn.

He falls out of my view. I feel like a cord connecting us has broken.

Then he runs back up to the top of the bowl and starts over. I'm mesmerized as he goes down, up, out of view, into view. He gets up a crazy momentum, and then he does it. He does the three-sixty perfectly.

On his next rise, he hops out of the bowl and someone else drops in. The guy goes to sit in the grass, just like that.

What I've just seen is art. No doubt about it. Beanie skater-guy is an artist.

I pull my sketchbook from my messenger bag and a charcoal from my box. I try to make something.

I start playing with shade, making swoops and swirls.

Ever since Holly got mad at me, I've felt full up of this energy that I couldn't get out because I didn't know how to make it right. It subsided, but now it's back. Nick has good reason to be pissed off, and I'm still on shaky ground with Holly.

This is even worse than before. As I work, I feel like I will burst. I really will.

I want art to take me away.

But charcoal on paper isn't doing anything. I flip to a new page and stare at it. This feels wrong. I want the squeeze of the spray paint can. The way you can't quite control the flow. The way the color is so alive, and so free.

I just look at the paper, thinking about blankness and choices. I could do anything. So why can't I do something?

Nick and I talk about coloring in the lines, filling them in. But who needs lines? I want to break completely free. I want to be out of bounds, out where it's all color and everything's beautiful, even when it's a mess.

If I sit still for one more minute, I think I really will burst.

I walk over to Palette, where it's slow. Oscar must be in back. Maye's at the main register.

"Hot chocolate craving?" she asks.

"In the worst way." We walk over to the espresso stand.

She pours the milk and starts to steam it. I want to talk to her about stuff, but I don't know where to start, exactly. Tell her I've ruined everything with my two best friends?

Tell her that school drives me nuts? Tell her that I'm afraid of messing up my life? That I want to be exactly like her, and can she tell me the steps to take to get there?

Just being quiet is all I have to do, because she asks, "Are you okay?"

"I'm stressed out is all," I say. But I do want to talk. I can't dismiss this energy. "Are you ever just sick of being yourself?"

She turns off the steamer and stirs my drink. I reconsider the question. "Duh, of course you're not sick of yourself. You're awesome."

She lets out a breath, hands me my drink. "You think I'm awesome? That's so sweet, Vanessa."

"It's just true. You're kind of a role model for me, I guess."

"Well, I'm glad we met too. You're so much cooler than I was at your age," she says. "You're so far ahead with your art. I can tell just by the way you talk about it."

"I doubt that."

"You're right on track," she says. "You're really gonna be something. By the time you're my age, I have a feeling you'll be doing way better than little shows at the Ballard Collective."

"I'd be thrilled with shows at the Ballard Collective. I hope I can get there."

"You can," she says. "You will. Just trust yourself."

I take my hot chocolate and walk home, teeny buds of inspiration blooming through the electric storm inside me.

* * *

I go to my room, throw on my splattered tank dress, and run to the garage to spray again.

This time, I use the wall. The inside of the garage. First, I move my drop cloth to cover up the parts of Grampie's Chevy that are closest to where I'm working. He'd never forgive me if I messed up his car.

There's not enough wall to get out everything I'm feeling.

Red hearts. Holly. Blue question marks. Nick. Sweeps of black with a nozzle that make it look gray. Spraying and spraying and spraying.

I stand back and look at my work, which didn't feel like work at all. It felt like the burst I needed. It's all about worry over Nick and Holly, and that's real, but there's this other thing in me now. This thing that says my trouble with them is not undoable.

I grab the yellow and make a sun up in the corner.

The spray paint got all over my dress. I smile to myself over adding new splotches to it from doing something that felt so right. It also got on my skin. So I cool down with a long shower.

Mom orders pizza for dinner, and when it shows up I join her and Grampie in the kitchen. I don't know what will happen when one of them sees the garage. Maybe I should just tell them?

Grampie talks about the Greenwood Car Show, which is coming up. It's kind of the highlight of his year. One of the few times he actually shows off his Chevy.

Eventually, Grampie says, "So how's my workin' girl? You enjoying punching the ol' time card?"

"Yep," I say. "I really like it."

"That's good, kiddo," he says. "It's good to earn some money."

"Abso-snootly," I say. I'm trying really hard to not let on that, really, I feel as if I'm losing my friends.

"Yeah," Mom says. "You haven't been around much. You and Nick hung out today, right?"

"We went to the mall," I say. "With Holly." It should be happy news.

"That's great!"

"Yeah."

"I'm assuming she's forgiven you."

"I'm not sure. Things are going really well between her and Wilson now, so she's happy. And she said I was the first person she wanted to tell. But I'm not sure if everything's really quite right between us yet." I stop. I don't want to rehash this.

"Things like that can take time, Nessie," Mom says. "But she's like a sister to you. You need to talk until it's all out."

Grampie nods. "Life's too short for regrets."

If anyone else said that, I'd mock it.

"I'll try," I say.

We munch on our pizza, and I feel a little bit okay.

I still have my family, and now I have a new kind of color.

That night, in bed, I let my thoughts drift back to what I said about Nick today. I'm not sure why I said it. I don't think of him as a girl. Not at all. He's Nick.

All I wanted to do was show that lady that boundaries are nothing. That everything doesn't have to be all neat and organized and normal to be good. Like a Pollock painting, all messy and beautiful and saying something just by being there.

Life can be like that.

Can't life be like that?

Thirteen

I walk to school on Monday wearing an orange string, only two steps up from black.

Nick isn't waiting at the door.

That's a huge first.

I think of Grampie and what he said about regrets.

That applies to Nick as much as it does to Holly.

I find him at lunch, at some random table.

He keeps his head down.

"Nick, look," I say. "Look at me."

He doesn't.

"I don't want things to be messed up between us. Look, Nick." I hold up my wrist. "Orange." He looks at me now. "I'm sorry for being stupid yesterday," I whisper.

"You should be," he says.

"I am," I say. "I really am, Nick."

He puts his head back down.

I spend lunch in the library, looking through a Jackson Pollock biography.

It's almost impossible to sit still the rest of the day.

I am not this person.

This person in a box, waiting for something to happen.

After school, Nick's waiting by my locker.

He looks right at me this time. "I think I accept your apology. Lunch was miserable without you. I can't handle knowing you're in an orange zone."

I grab him in a hug. "I really am sorry," I say into his hair. I breathe out.

"I know. It's okay. Just don't ever say that again."

There's still a twinge in his voice, but I ignore it. I have to. I cannot take a confrontation right now. If he's over it, then I'm over it.

I pull back feeling lighter. We can get back to normal. "We should do our hair this week."

He's saying I'm naive. And maybe he's right. Maybe I can't change anything.

But then what are we all doing? Why bother at all?

"I just think . . . Not everyone is fine with a gay guy. And not everyone is fine with a girl like you, either. But we've got it pretty good. We have fun together. Isn't that enough for now?"

For now. When will now become then, the time that's always somewhere out there in front of us? I hate this feeling, like I need something different, something he's not ready for. But that doesn't mean I'm not ready for it. To explode.

Because I am.

I can handle what comes.

What fun is living within boundaries?

There might be a few casualties along the way, but I have to do what I feel is right. It feels like he's asking me to hold back. Stay inside the lines.

I can do what I want. Nothing's stopping me. No one's telling me what to do.

"No," I say. "That's definitely not enough for me."

I push past Nick.

He follows me outside. "Vanessa!" I turn around automatically. "You know what? It's time for you to stop messing with my life. And Holly's. What about your own life? What are you even doing for the spring show?"

"I've barely even thought about the spring show, Nick."

"Exactly."

It's like he releases me with his gaze. I get to my bike and ride around until dark, trying to pedal out this lightning inside me.

Tuesday morning, I pack my messenger bag with supplies.

Not for school.

I try to look like everything's normal. I give Mom a hug before I get in the shower. I tell Grampie to have a great day in the garden.

Then I do what I want to do.

Picking a place is the hardest part. I don't want to destroy anything. I just want to create art that people can see.

I head to the park near school, before anyone's around.

I use the basketball blacktop.

My symbol: a lightning bolt. A field full of zap.

Everything I've been feeling lately is like electricity. Shooting through me, making my life light up. Strong, flashing, bright.

Squeezing it out in purple on the blacktop feels even better than practicing in the garage. I feel so alive. This color cannot be contained.

I make at least twenty before my breathing calms and I feel okay.

It's nearly impossible to force myself to go sit through a day of school after that, but I do it.

All week, I visit the park in the morning, and during lunch, I hide in the library with Jackson Pollock.

Grampie notices the garage at some point on Wednesday.

Over dinner, he says to Mom, "Have you seen Nessie's latest masterpiece?"

She shakes her head. "Go get it, Nessie. I want to see."

I realize what Grampie means, and I panic. But he doesn't seem mad.

He says, "It's in the garage. It looks almost like a Pollock. But more . . . girly."

It's probably the best thing anyone's said about me in months.

"Thanks, Grampie."

Mom goes out to look, right in the middle of dinner.

Grampie and I keep eating. When she gets back, she says, "Wow. I'm just glad your hair never got quite that colorful."

I guess I'm allowed to spray-paint the garage. Cool.

More than cool, now I know what to do for the school art show.

* * *

Holly calls on Thursday after school. "I got a dress," she says. "I just wanted you to know. Nick and I went shopping last night."

I don't know what to say.

"It felt weird not to tell you. It felt weird not to have you there."

It's more than weird. It's me losing my friends. I should have been there. I should be listening to every little thing she has to say about Wilson and the dance and the rest of her life.

I'm crying but I don't want her to know. Fortunately, she keeps talking.

"He's just worried about you, you know? He's not mad. I'm not mad. We both think you've gotten a little . . . out of control. We needed some space."

I created that space. I know it. But I'm not quite sure how to close the gap.

I gulp and breathe deeply. "So, Wilson asked you?"

"Monday night at rehearsal, yep."

"You're getting exactly what you want. That's great."

"What is it you want, Nessie?"

"I want . . . to live without boundaries."

She sighs. "What does that even mean?"

It means her kind of life is too small for me. Nick's kind of patience is too much for me. "It means . . . growing up."

"We all are, Ness. I'm gonna go practice."

We hang up, and I think about it. Maybe we're all growing up, but why am I the only one who wants it to happen faster?

The school show's on Friday night. I signed up a long time ago to help with setup after school. I won't let Mr. Smith down.

During lunch, I get a text from James. My ID is ready, and we arrange a meeting at the skate park at six-thirty.

Perfect. I had no intention of going to the actual art show anyway. I haven't even told Mom or Grampie about it. Other parents will be there, and Smith, of course, and all the kids who take art.

I'll let my art speak for me.

Other people are setting up too, including Jewel and Alice. They're in charge of the cheese cubes. They look really happy. Maybe I really am over Jewel. There's definitely less of a sting.

It's my job to hang up the work on the walls in the lobby and in the small gallery room next to the office.

Jewel's done some photos. They're perfect, of course. Black-and-white shots of flowers and fruit down at Pike Place Market.

Alice made a collage out of old magazines. Lots of

nature. I like what she did; you can tell the pieces are trees and rivers and rocks, but she's put them together in a really interesting way, so they're something new.

I hang Nick's rebel Prince Charming sketches. He did it all himself. Pencil, ink, color. The character has a personality, just in the lopsided way his crown sits on his swoopy hair. Nick's gotten really good. How did I not notice that before now?

I finish, shut the door, and get to work on my own entry.

I brought all my colors, and three different tips, but sharp pink feels the most right. Hot pink, like my hair.

I didn't have space to pack a drop cloth, but I kept everyone else's work away from one wall.

I go crazy.

I spray and, just like the other times, it's like the can is part of my body, an extension of my thoughts. Then my thoughts go blank and I'm feeling, making something.

Doing this.

It doesn't take long.

I don't care if I win the art show. This isn't about some art show. If I want more people to see it, I can make my own show on the street somewhere.

But this is more important than winning.

Fourteen

When I get to the skate park, I'm a little late because I got so wrapped up in painting, but James isn't there yet. I sit on the same bench I tried to use for drawing last weekend. How far I've come since then. How much farther I'm going.

I can't even sit still right now, so I walk over to the skate bowl, do laps around it.

He shows up, in the usual jeans and his Vespa jacket with a patch on the shoulder. It's olive green, and really sets off his blond surfer hair.

I almost leap into the air as he walks up to me. For a

second, I wonder if I should take him to the art show, go after all. Show off what I did.

He taps his jeans pocket. "Got somethin' for ya." He pulls the ID out. "Here you go, Jennifer."

My new name is Jennifer Jones, and I turned twenty-one about three weeks ago. He's not so imaginative with the names, but I'll give James this much: it looks authentic.

"Thanks." I'm grinning.

"There's something I've been thinking about asking you, actually." He's been thinking about me?

"Shoot," I say.

"Miss August dropped out."

It takes only a second for me to realize what he's talking about. "The calendar?"

"Yeah, so I need someone last-minute to fill in, and you're a natural in front of the camera. Want to do it? Pays two hundred bucks. We could call the ID square, and you'd still make some cash."

Do I want to pose as a pinup girl in the same calendar that Maye's in, for James? Yes! Yes! Yes! So much better than showing him my painting.

"Sure," I say. "Sounds fun."

"Great, 'cause my deadline is looming and I've got time to kill right now."

Right now? I have nothing to wear. "Wardrobe?"

"Junk shop in Fremont's open."

It's perfect. "Let's go."

"All right," he says. "Ever ridden a Vespa?"

"First time for everything," I say. *You gotta live*.

"I like your attitude." He leads me back toward his apartment, holding his skateboard, and I feel a zing: this is our *second* adventure together.

We go into the garage, walk over to a scooter that's part blue, part orange, all used, and a bit rusted, but still decidedly adorable. "It's my monster scooter. Like Frankenstein," he says. "Made from a bunch of different parts."

James hands me a white helmet, shows me how to strap it under my chin, then fastens his own: a little black shell with a silver star on top that doesn't look like it would protect anything in a crash, much less a skull. That's okay, though; nothing will happen to us. Nothing can. I've waited too long to feel this free.

He drops the scooter off its kickstand, straddles it, and says, "Get on." I situate myself onto the tiny bit of seat left behind him, not sure what to do with my hands. He reaches back and pulls me so that I'm hugging him. "You'll want to hold on." I could've told him that much. I slide my arms around him.

When he first turns the throttle, we lurch forward, and I love the way my body presses into his back.

Then we get out of the garage, out of the alley, onto Market Street, and we really go.

I keep my arms around him and watch my world go by

from this whole new perspective. I know we're not going crazy fast—it's only a scooter—but it feels as if we're zooming. The air whips at my face, waking me up.

I don't care if we never get to Fremont, but, finally, we dismount, take off our helmets, and put them on the scooter seat.

"Like the ride?" James asks.

"Oh, yeah." Can he tell how much? Is he picking up this vibe I'm sending? It feels like we are the only two creatures on this weird planet. How can he *not* be feeling that? And I haven't even told him about my new spray-paint thing yet. He doesn't even know who I really am.

The junk shop has a window display up for Easter, a four-foot-tall white bunny in all his fuzzy glory wearing a bow tie, with plastic eggs all around. James gets to work browsing the racks. I follow his lead.

It's like he's the artist and I'm his canvas. Or, even, his muse.

He seems to forget I'm even there, until he holds up a black-and-white polka-dot bikini, the kind with boy-shorts and a halter top. "Perfecto!"

"Bikini?"

"You're Miss August. It *has* to be a bikini." His eyes sparkle.

"Fine by me."

I'm pale, but that's kind of retro. Pale is kind of pinup girl.

He holds the top up to me and definitely sizes up my chest, which isn't nearly as spectacular as Maye's, but I know I'm perky. He shoves the bikini at me and goes to look for shoes, still on a mission. All lit up.

I hover around a stack of old magazines, thinking I'll take a minute to study the poses. I find the one I like, a cover girl posing by a bicycle that looks a lot like mine. She stands with her legs together and bent, with her arms up over her head as if she's about to dive into a pool that isn't there.

I'm smiling at the image when someone taps my shoulder.

Jewel. "Hey, Vanessa."

I'm surprised to see him, though when I think about it, I shouldn't be. We came here to get my Halloween Bloodbath prom-queen dress.

"Hey." Did he see me with James? Does he know I'm not alone? Is he alone? Do I care?

"Find anything good?"

I show him the magazine.

"Cool. Is that for an art project or something?"

I nod. "Something. Hey, shouldn't you be at the art show?"

"I'm on my way. Wanted to pick up this polka-dot tie I saw here last weekend, but it's gone." He looks toward the door, then back to me. "Shouldn't you be there too?"

My mind flashes to what I left there. I wonder how he'll react. I wonder how everyone will react. "I'm not . . ."

I see James walking toward us before Jewel realizes anyone's behind him. "I'm not going to the show. I'm busy with . . ." James reaches us, and I grab his arm. "Him."

James is oblivious to the importance of this moment. Something clouds over Jewel for a second. He looks at the bikini in James's hands, then at me.

"This is James," I say. "And this is Jewel."

"Hey."

"Hey." James barely even looks at Jewel. "Let's get a move on."

Jewel's gaze catches my eye. "We'll miss you at the show."

I nod. "Have fun. Good luck."

He heads toward the door without looking back.

After Jewel's gone, James and I flip through vintage sunglasses. I check out old jewelry. Then I spot a pair of saddle shoes. "I want these."

"Cool," he says. "Just to have, I mean. Not right for the shoot. You'll have to do barefoot. Can you paint your toes?"

"No problem."

"Great. We can stop by Maye's, actually. Get the right color and maybe borrow her hair stuff too, and makeup. Accessories."

"Sure." I don't mention that I have all that stuff at my

147

house. How would I explain him to Grampie? Plus, I *want* to stop by Maye's; I want the whole world to know I'm doing this with James.

We buy the bikini—he pays; I would've if he'd asked, 'cause I'm planning on keeping it—then hop back onto the scooter.

Maye lives right here in Fremont, just on the other side of the bridge, it turns out. She's got a mother-in-law apartment, I think that's what they're called, over someone's garage. The place looks cozy, with an A-frame roof, white lace curtains, and fairy lights around the front windows.

James goes up the wooden steps and taps on the door.

Maye opens it in her bathrobe. I smell tomato sauce cooking. Today's the day the other Palette staffers work so Maye and Oscar have a day off to spend together.

She registers surprise at seeing me, but says only, "Hey." She turns to James. "I guess you did ask her to do it."

"Yep, you're looking at Miss August."

I do a little curtsy.

She doesn't invite us in. Which seems rude. Not like her. And why did she know about him asking me to be in the calendar before I did?

"We need to borrow some nail polish," I say. I wiggle my fingers at her.

"And one of your scarves for her hair," James adds, and pushes his way in. Maye lets him, and I follow.

Her place is sort of like James's. It's decorated much

better, but it's one room with a kitchen. There are fabric scraps and yarn in plastic containers in one corner, and stuffing. Bowls full of buttons, beads, sequins. The makings for her dolls take up most of the space.

The supplies are the first thing I notice. Then I see Oscar on her bed, wrapped in a white sheet.

He's sitting up, and his smile is kind of like the fake one the Dazzle lady put on. "Not the best timing."

James is at the sink pulling strings of spaghetti out of Maye's strainer.

Maye roots around in her top drawer—the dresser looks kind of old Hollywood; I love it—and hands me a bottle of pale pink nail polish and a red and white polka-dot scarf, the perfect match to the bikini.

"That's our dinner," she says to James.

"You mind?" he asks, chewing.

Clearly, she does. She shoots a look to Oscar, who's sitting up on the bed forming a toga. "Guess not," she says.

"Great." James grabs a bowl from the counter, and fills it.

She's got only one chair and it's covered with clothes, so James goes to sit on the corner of the bed, where Oscar is still naked under that sheet.

"Vanessa," Maye says, and moves forward so that I'm forced to step backward onto her little porch.

She shuts the door behind us, and there we are.

"Don't worry," I say. "I'm not scarred by seeing Oscar in your bed."

"That's not it," she says, "though, yeah, it's not cool that you guys just showed up. The timing could've been worse."

I can imagine.

"Sorry." It's strange to think about. Very new, for me. None of my other friends even have sex, let alone in their own little apartment. While it's still semi-light outside.

"Look, Vanessa," she says. "Do you know what you're doing with James?"

"I'm doing the calendar, same as you." It comes out sounding venomous. Why do I feel the need to defend this? "But it sounds like you already knew that."

"I told him not to ask you," she says. "I think it'll look silly, a sixteen-year-old girl . . . it's not right for you. James should know. He's too old for you, Vanessa, and you're not old enough for this calendar." I feel ten times the annoyance I felt toward the Dazzle lady.

"I can handle it." I can, and I will.

"What's your deal with wanting to be older?" she asks. Just like Nick did. And Mom. What is with everyone not believing in me? Who says I can't hang out with James, or date him? "You're adorable, and you have so much in front of you. So much time for guys like James. Don't do anything with him. I'm telling you, it's not right."

"You have no idea what I'm capable of." I'm ready for anything. I'm lightning, shining out.

"That's what worries me. Bad things can happen,

Vanessa. A guy like James. He's fun. He's good at heart, but he has no business with you."

"Actually," I say, "I think it's pretty clear that he does."

He opens the door then and pushes past Maye, which forces her back into her place, the porch being so small. He holds up a plastic grocery bag loaded with her accessories. "Ready to do this?"

"Totally," I say.

I turn my back on Maye, and lead James down the steps.

Helmets on, we zoom back over the Fremont Bridge, through the arty strip, past the restaurants and coffee shops into Ballard, where the air is salty, and down the alley to the Vespa shop and James's place. I keep my arms tightly around his waist the whole ride, and even rest my cheek on his back. I'm going to keep taking steps toward him until we mesh completely. I will not leave quietly tonight.

When we get there, he drives into the garage and parks the monster scooter next to one that's completely taken apart. It looks like a surgery patient on the operating table. He helps me off with my helmet, and I feel like he's revealing the real me.

I'm still wearing my bag, which holds the bikini and Maye's supplies.

"I'm gonna set up the camera and everything," he says. "Why don't you go up and change, paint your nails, do your makeup, whatever, and meet me back down here?"

"We're shooting in the garage?"

"Sure, Vespas are the perfect accessory."

I love this idea. "Awesome," I say.

He tosses me his keys so that I can go upstairs. I have to go back outside first, to his fire-escape stairs. In the garage, there's a scent of metal and oil, and outside, there's the sea-water smell.

I go up the stairs and use James's key. It's easy to imagine this being my life: my own key to this apartment, which I would spruce up—so many white walls just begging for me! James would work downstairs while I did my thing upstairs, and then we'd meet at night.

He definitely hasn't cleaned since I was last here. I pull out the nail polish, lipstick, head scarf, and bikini. I put on the bikini first, feeling so charged and zingy because, for a moment, I am naked in James's apartment, the same way Oscar is naked in Maye's.

The suit bottom fits fine, but I don't quite fill out the top. I bend over to readjust the girls, and manage to make it less obvious. If I keep my back arched so that my chest stays up, I should be fine.

Next, I go into the bathroom to tie the scarf. The sink is full of tiny hairs, which must be from shaving. A cardboard box next to the sink serves as a trash can, and a CD rack on the floor is the medicine cabinet. I notice all the boy things, which, actually, aren't many—shaving cream and razors, deodorant, an extra bar of grocery-store-brand soap—and among them, one tube of pink deodorant. *An old girlfriend's.*

I want that to be mine. I want to be the one keeping my getting-ready-for-the-day supplies in his bathroom.

I tie the scarf on like a headband, which looks so adorable that I might start wearing it regularly. Then I grab toilet paper to put under my toes and go back to the main room. I feel like someone should make a portrait of me at this moment, sitting on James's floor in the teeny-weeny polka-dot bikini, my hair all retro, painting my nails. Thank the Goddess I shaved my legs this morning.

While I wait for my toes to dry, I consider everything that's going on. I'm breaking free. I'm following what I want to do, and it means I get a guy like James to notice me, which is so much better than a guy like Mike Corrigan. Than any high school boy. Than even Jewel.

I knew that working at Palette would change things. It's happening.

Once my nails are dry, I gather up my clothes and stuff them into my messenger bag, sling the bag on, zip up my boots, and go back downstairs. I'm cold in the bikini, but not shivering.

* * *

James chuckles as I pull a face. I'm sitting atop someone's green Vespa in front of his tool wall.

We've been shooting for about twenty minutes, and I'm
having the time of my life. It's like the ID session, but this
time I really get to ham it up, channeling Maye and the
photo of my grandmother sitting on Grampie's Chevy, and
every other strong woman I can think of.

I can't help but think James is having a blast too. He
laughs as he clicks away.

"I'm so glad you agreed to do this, Vanessa," he says,
holding the camera at his side for a minute.

When he says my name, I understand what people
mean about melting around someone they love. "Me too."

He picks up the camera again and gets what must
be the most natural shots of the session, me relishing the
moment. I'm sure the look on my face is totally serene.

I've been mostly sitting up straight on the Vespa's seat,
so I decide to lean over and grab the handlebars, to make it
look like I'm driving. I try to remember how the pinup girls
shaped their bodies.

As I bend, the bikini top gapes a little. I look up at
James, and in a split second before he looks away, I know
that he's looking at my body, and I know that he likes what
he sees.

So I don't fix the top.

James takes a few more photos, then holds the camera
in front of himself, fiddling with the settings.

I seize this moment. I reach around to the bikini top's closure, and undo it.

James looks up. He watches. He's absolutely still, and I know this is going to happen.

He puts the camera down on the workbench, next to the helmets and his jacket, my boots on the floor.

He's so close to me now. And walking closer.

I pull the top completely off, let it fall to the greasy floor. I stand up, take a step toward James, and we're together. We're kissing.

It was that easy.

Nothing has ever felt this good—not even kissing Jewel.

His hands are on my bare back, and I feel myself pressed into his chest. He takes off his top.

Skin against skin. Softer than I'd ever imagined.

We are finally melting together.

"Let's go upstairs," I mumble into his hair.

He takes my hand, grabs his jacket from the bench, and hands it to me.

I put it on.

We kiss again. We can walk only three steps before we *need* to keep kissing.

Going up the stairs, we stop twice.

Time stands still, and we're in his place, and we're still kissing like crazy, and I take the jacket off. He kicks off his Chucks and pulls off his jeans, so we're both basically in underwear. His is the sexy kind that's like tight boxers. The bulge is definitely there.

Exactly how do we get these last pieces of clothing off? And how do I bring up the condom issue?

We keep kissing, and he presses me up against the sink, and it's cold on my skin, and he's heavy up against me, and I feel him on my leg, right there, and his arms are strong on either side of me, and I don't want it to, but it feels like he's trapping me. I'm letting him. I asked him to. I want this.

Maye's words, my mom's, and Nick's, echo. *Don't grow up too fast*, they all said, and maybe this is what they meant, but how can something that felt so amazing one second ago cross this line to feeling locked up?

No. This is fine. I started this. We'll stop whenever I say so.

"I'll get something," he says, and moves to walk to the bathroom for what I hope is a condom. When he steps away, it leaves me chilled. Goose bumps.

I take the chance to get on the mattress, under the covers. As I'm wiggling around trying to find the right way of lying there, my leg swipes something cold. At first, the image of an eel pops to mind.

Just as he's coming out of the bathroom with his hand cupped—it must be a condom inside, yes—I reach down and feel a necklace.

I pull it out from under the covers, and see that it has a dainty jeweled ballet slipper hanging from it.

Wait.

He's walking toward me, but I feel myself pulling the sheet around me, shoving the necklace back down.

I can't go through with this knowing there's another girl's necklace in the bed—and that it's probably her deodorant in the bathroom. Not as much of an ex-girlfriend as I thought, maybe.

"James." I will my voice not to crack. "I have to go."

He sits at the edge of the bed. "Relax. Everything's okay. We can slow down," he says. "I thought we'd finish up here and then go use your ID, but if you need more time, we can stay in all night."

I just look at him. I want to want that. But I'm not sure anymore.

I reach down for the necklace, hold it up.

"She's not someone I'm serious about," he says. "Just a girl I know."

"Oh." I nod. So, am I just a girl too? I can't ask, because I don't want to know the answer.

"You're not cool with this, are you?"

"Not tonight," I say. I flash to a scene where I tell Maye about this, and she's proud that I didn't ignore the necklace. She thinks I did the right thing. Holly would tell me to get out of here, and quick. Nick? Same thing.

I pull my clothes back up around me while he drags on his jeans. "Are you sure?" he asks.

I nod and go to the door. "See ya," I mumble. I know

157

he'll go out by himself. Or meet up with the necklace girl. Or someone else.

I walk home, trying not to think. I don't know what to think anymore.

Mom and Grampie are nowhere to be seen when I get home. I go straight to bed, stopping only to change out of my clothes—the bikini underneath—and into my splattered tank dress.

The last images in my mind before I fall asleep are of myself on that Vespa, barely dressed. Trying to look sexy.

What was I thinking? Mom and Grampie could come across the calendar. Anyone could. It's not art. Not at all. It's a private moment that probably never should've happened.

I have to get out of the calendar.

Fifteen

I'm scheduled to work on Saturday, but I'm still asleep when Nick calls. I hadn't looked at my phone last night, but now I see that he called twice. I click to him. "What's up?"

"Um, hello? Badass?" Oh. "You graffitied the school." At least he's talking to me. It's been almost a week since our fight.

"Just that one wall."

"Uh-huh. And the blacktop at the park—I guess you did that, too? This is your big project? This is what you came up with?"

When he puts it like that, I realize I barely even

thought about the show. I wanted to do my best project ever. Then I got distracted. "I don't care about some dumb school art show," I say. "It just felt good to do. It felt . . . real."

"It's really getting you in trouble, that's for sure."

"I mean, it's just one wall. Is Smith mad?"

"He seemed okay, actually. But I do know the office called your house and left a message last night."

As if on cue, Mom opens my door. She does not look cheery.

"Gotta go. I'll call you back." I click the phone off. "Hi, Mom."

"That's it? 'Hi, Mom'? Nessie, what were you thinking?"

"It's art, Mom. It's what I was feeling." Even as I say that, it doesn't sound quite right.

"It's multicolored lightning bolts on the wall of the school."

"Right. My art show entry."

"And they said that your so-called art matched some graffiti at the park over by the school? Was that yours, too?"

I can't defend the park as easily. I don't know how to explain that it felt like energy bursting out of me. That I didn't know where else to put that energy.

So I just look her in the eye and nod, wishing she could read my mind. For the first time, I think maybe I need help figuring out where my energy should go.

"You're going over there today to paint over that wall.

And the school is punishing you. You're not allowed to go to Spring Semi."

I push out a laugh. "As if I want to go to Spring Semi. That's fine."

"And I'm punishing you too."

I wait for it.

"You've had your last shift at Palette. And you'll spend spring break at home."

I start to shake inside. She can't take that away. Oscar. Maye. James. "But—"

"Working there was a privilege."

"A privilege where I get paid!"

"Most of your check will be going to the Parks Department, to cover the cost of the new blacktop they need to put down to fix your mess on the basketball court. You know the job was never about getting paid. You just wanted to be around those artist people."

"Those artist people are my friends."

"Holly's your friend. Nick. Think about that. Think about us."

I can't even look at her.

"You're due at the school in one hour. I'm dropping you off, and then I'm picking you up and you are not leaving this house for the rest of break. We'll stop at the hardware store on the way for paint."

With that, she shuts the door and leaves me feeling once again like I might explode. I can't handle sitting here quietly.

This kind of energy is what's gotten me where I am. Which is . . . where? Noticed for the wrong things, the ones I'm not proud of. My messy insides.

What, what's *wrong*? I fall back on the bed.

When I got what I thought I wanted with James, I wasn't ready. I'm nowhere near ready for my own art show, either. I need to face it—I'm not ready. For a lot of things.

What a mess I've made.

I call Palette and leave a message for Oscar, telling him I'm sick and won't be in. When I hang up, I start to cry. I'm glad I don't have to lie directly to him.

Then I call Nick back and pace my room while we talk. "I'm not allowed to go to the Spring Semi. I'm sorry. I can't be your date."

He says, "I don't really want to go."

"But, you said . . ."

"Okay." He breathes out. "I do want to go. I want to want to, anyway. It would make me feel . . . normal."

This again? "You're not normal, Nick. . . . Maybe no one is. Maybe that's what's really beautiful in life."

He's quiet for a few seconds. I need to practice doing that. Thinking before I say and do things. "You could be right."

* * *

When I get to the gallery room, I see that Alice and Jewel each got ribbons. Jewel won Best Sophomore Work and Alice won Peers' Choice.

My wall, my bright wall, a version of what I did in the garage that day, is the most alive thing in the room. I could have done better. I'm not nearly practiced enough at spraying yet.

I wasted the chance to show people something good. Something I'd actually put some real thought into, instead of just a burst of energy.

I'm embarrassed looking at it, but painting chalk white over my bolts still feels like erasing part of myself.

Mr. Smith shows up when I'm almost done.

I stop and try to smile. "You're checking on me?"

He runs his hand through his thinning hair, that way that he does. "I wanted to talk to you."

"You and everybody else."

He looks straight at me. That's one of the things I've always appreciated about Mr. Smith. "I think you've been looking for yourself, Vanessa."

"I guess . . . but not anymore."

"I've noticed changes in you. But I don't think anyone ever fully knows themselves. If we did, what would be the point of continuing to make art?"

He nods to the wall, where only a tiny bit of my work remains. "Your piece was kind of like a Pollock. I know how much you like him. But it was also kind of a mess, Vanessa."

"I thought I was breaking out of bounds, just like he did."

Mr. Smith wrinkles his nose. "How was he out of bounds?"

"He was free. To make a beautiful mess."

"But he still had boundaries."

I can tell Smith wants me to say something.

I think about it.

And I realize. "The canvas."

"The canvas. His was big, but it was still there. He still worked in a context."

"But I wanted . . . to be beyond that."

"Do you think that's possible?"

I'm silent. Trying to think.

"There are always boundaries," he says. "This time, yours was this wall."

"But I'm . . . a continuation of the art. It's a living thing. It's me."

"You're an artist, yes. But we're all just people. Did you ever think that maybe we need boundaries, we need the lines?"

I shake my head, looking him in the eye. "Absolutely not. I think people are free. At least, I know they should be."

"But if we don't have the lines, how does anyone know where to look? If the whole world was a Pollock painting, then would any of it really look beautiful? He needed a canvas. The lines. So do you."

I don't have an answer for that. Maybe he's right. Maybe art is only beautiful when there's also not-art.

He picks up a paintbrush to help me finish just as Mom walks in. "Hello, Ms. Almond."

I start packing up the paintbrush and the tray. She shakes his hand. "Thanks for being here."

"No problem," he says. "I hope you'll let Vanessa consider the summer job with the elementary kids."

"Duh," I say. "I'm obviously not the best role model."

Mom doesn't say anything.

But Smith goes on, "Oh, I think you can be." He takes the bag of supplies from me.

"Thank you, Mr. Smith. We'll see." Mom is formal.

She's angry. I want to tell her it's just a wall. It was art. But I also know it's not true. It was about wanting to be noticed, too—but not like this. I shake my head. I can't think about this anymore.

I follow her to her Jeep, and we ride silently home.

I'm still thinking about it the next day.

The spray paint can't be all bad. It felt too good. Maybe I do need a canvas. Like Mr. Smith said. There's no rule saying I can't spray a canvas.

I need to go tell Oscar I'm done. Maye, too. Apologize.

Mom's in the garden with Grampie. I walk out there, enjoying the damp grass under my bare feet.

165

"I know I'm not supposed to go anywhere, but I need to quit Palette in person."

Mom stands up. "I'll come with you. I need to pick up laundry detergent. We'll stop at the store."

"I really think I need to do this alone."

"I'll wait outside, but, Vanessa, I mean it when I say you are grounded over this break."

I have to accept that, I guess. "Let's go."

The drive to Palette feels like an important journey. Today I'm stepping back.

I stare at the cherry blossoms lining the block and wonder how I missed them yesterday. I'm paying attention now.

Oscar's behind the cash register, fiddling with the receipt tape.

I step up and wait for him to notice me.

"Fancy meeting you here," he says.

But I don't feel like playing around. I hold his gaze, not sure if I should go into details about why I'm quitting. I decide that it doesn't matter exactly why. He knows enough about me and James. "Thanks for everything, Oscar. I've really liked working here, but I just don't think it's the thing for me right now."

"You're quitting."

"I'm really, really sorry. I hope I'm not letting you and Maye down," I say. We're silent for a moment. "Are you surprised?"

"Not really," he says. "It's okay, Vanessa."

I don't want to bring up James. But I need Oscar to help me. "Just one more thing."

He raises his eyebrows.

"You know that calendar?"

He nods again. "Maye will get you out of it. She'll threaten to pull out herself if James doesn't get another model to fill in for you."

Just then, a girl comes through the door in jeans and a black hoodie. She walks up next to me. Oscar continues, "Right? You'll get Vanessa out of the calendar?"

Maye? I turn to look. It is her. "Where's your hair?" Her magnificent platinum dreads are completely gone.

"Took 'em out. Time for a change. They're just synthetic extensions."

"Oh."

I look at her. None of her tats are visible, and her real hair is kind of a mousy blond. But she's still her. Maybe a little more vulnerable.

I think maybe it is time to shave my head.

Then I think, no. I'd just be doing that for the attention. But it's time to go more natural with it.

She puts her hand on my shoulder. "I'll personally erase

your shoot from his camera, from his computer. Everywhere. It'll be like it never happened."

"Thanks," I say. "I owe you. Big-time." What I don't say, but I know she understands, is that she was right.

I know that now. I'm too young to be in that calendar. Just thinking about people ogling the moments before James and I almost . . . It's too much. Too real.

Maye gives me a hug. I walk out of there, a different girl from the one who walked in a few weeks ago hoping to change her life.

I got a change. Just not the one I was expecting.

When Mom and I get back from Palette, and then the drugstore, I carry my bag straight to my bathroom.

I cut the string off my wrist. That's the last time.

My art can be the statement.

I get out my supplies.

As I work on my hair, saturating every strand, I feel as if there's an imaginary breeze blowing.

Once I'm done, I find Mom sitting on the couch reading. She looks up. Cracks a smile. "Hey. You kind of look like me with your hair brown."

"I think so too. I like it." I settle in, our feet touching on the couch again. "I always thought . . ." I'm not sure how to put this. Mom waits. "I guess I always thought that if I looked like this, no one would notice me."

She laughs. "You are so much more than a hair color, Vanessa."

When I was looking in the mirror, what I saw was me. A girl figuring things out. A girl with a good family. Great friends. Lots to look forward to. "Do you think things will be different now?"

"Now? As opposed to when?"

"When I was trying to . . . break everything."

"You weren't trying to break anything. Everyone knows that. You just . . ."

"I got ahead of myself."

She nods. "What were those lightning bolts about, anyway?"

"I think I just felt like something . . . I needed to zap it out."

"You know, Nessie, real growth doesn't happen in a zap."

I nod. "It can be kind of sad, actually."

"Sad!" She puts her book on the coffee table.

"Have you noticed that Grampie's looking older?" My voice is cracking. "I sketch him. I want to remember him."

She nods. "Of course you'll remember him. Yes, Grampie's getting older. We all are. But he's not going anywhere anytime soon."

"But don't you think it's sad? Watching someone get

169

old? Like he's running out of time." It's how I've felt about her, too, now that I think about it.

She's quiet for a few seconds. "Actually, I think it's kind of beautiful. I had to deal with death young, Nessie. When my mom died, I was so angry."

I feel my throat tighten.

Mom continues. "But then I realized my life was still going. We all have a life span. Everything does. Maybe that's what I love so much about the salmon."

"I'm not following," I say. I'm still stuck wondering how you ever get over the death of your mother.

"Salmon travel incredible distances. They spawn in high altitudes, in fresh water. Only a few even grow out of the first stage of being an egg. The ones that do spend a few years out in the open ocean. Then they make amazing journeys—hundreds of miles—back to where they were spawned themselves. Pacific salmon, the ones we have here . . . they all die within a few days or weeks of spawning."

"But they've created the next generation."

"Exactly. I find comfort in that."

For a second, I think she means that part of her died when she had me. But it hits me that she's saying there's something good in knowing that the cycle continues. That the things that happen out in the wide ocean are as varied as anyone can imagine.

Maybe this is why she likes working at the docks so

much. I bet it reminds her of this belief I never even knew she had.

"Mom?"

"Hmm?"

"Thank you for making my life so good."

She smiles. "We did it together, Nessie."

"Us and Grampie."

"Yes. But your own life, now, that's mostly up to you."

She's right. I'll make plenty of decisions in my lifetime. I've got so much time left. "What if I said I want to teach those kids this summer?"

"I think Mr. Smith is probably right. You'd be good at it."

I actually believe her.

That's enough.

Spring break was quiet. I got to interview for the art camp job. Did some gardening with Grampie.

School on Monday is a blur. People stare at me all day. This time, it's because I've stopped looking like a work of art. Could be the graffiti drama too. Who cares?

"There's a shock to not being shocking," I tell Mr. Smith when he asks me to stay after workshop.

"Interesting observation," he says. "Did you think all art had to be about shock?"

I consider. "Maybe I did."

"What do you think now? What makes art into art?"

I want to quip, say "I wish I knew," something like that. But instead I just think. I breathe. "I think . . . I'm not sure. I think it might . . . defy definition. But what I know is, I don't want to stop looking for that definition. I like the way it feels to create."

He nods. "Another interesting thought. You are becoming a real student of life, Vanessa."

A *student of life.* I like that. "Thanks. And I'm excited to become a teacher this summer, too."

"Excellent. That's what I wanted to talk to you about. The training program starts next week. The elementary school called to say they'd love to have you." He hands me a schedule. The tardy bell rings. Another class is filling the room.

Mr. Smith writes me a late pass and I walk to gym, glad that I have the teacher training coming up. Glad that I'm going to take the time to learn how to do this summer job well.

When I get my one and only Palette check in the mail, Mom cashes it for me. She keeps most of the cash and writes the check for the blacktop. The rest she hands over. "You did earn it."

Even though I'm not going to use it, I still owe James for the ID.

I take the money, feeling stupid that I already spent it on something so pointless.

After school the next day, I pedal over to the Vespa shop.

Part of me wants him to be there, and part of me hopes I can just leave the envelope.

It feels like a big moment, but I tell myself: It'll pass. This is something I have to do. James was never anything but good to me.

He's there, taking a break, reading the *Weekly*, sitting on the workbench with an energy drink next to him.

"Hey."

He looks up. "I like the hair." He smiles, and for a few seconds, I want to sink. But I need to stay clear.

"Thanks." I pull the envelope out of my bag. "Here's what I owe you for the . . . for Jennifer."

He takes it. "I wish I didn't need the cash. I mean, we never even got to use your ID. . . . Seems like a waste."

"It's okay," I say. What did I really waste here?

"You can still use it. Just—I'm sorry, but . . . not with me."

Wow. It never even occurred to me that he'd think I still wanted to hang out with him. To . . . whatever. "I know that, James."

But then I realize I have no idea what he's thinking. "I mean, why not with you?"

"You pulled out of the calendar, Vanessa. Maye told me how it made you uncomfortable. You and I . . . we had fun together for a minute. That's all it was. We're in different places. I shouldn't have gone there with you."

I take a deep breath because this burns. This is rejection. I thought I was coming here to tell him goodbye, but this feels like he's telling me to go away. There's a distinction. Tears form before I can stop them. "Sorry I wasted your time."

"Don't think of it like that," he says. "Think of it like . . . a view to . . . your future."

I wipe at my cheeks and turn to go.

As I climb back on my bike and pedal away, I don't think that future is the one I want at all.

In the park, I sit atop my cruiser on the basketball blacktop. My bolts are still there.

Seems silly now, but I'm not sad that I did it. Not exactly. I only wish I hadn't done it in public. I just thought people needed to see what I was feeling. But maybe I'm the only one who needed to see.

Mom doesn't know, but I called the Parks Department. Starting this weekend, I'm on a volunteer cleanup crew. They even said I could work at the skate park.

* * *

The Sunday after Spring Semi, my punishments are over. I'm allowed to go out, and the sun is glorious. I text Nick and Holly. Tell them I have a treat.

It's too warm for my boots, so I put on my saddle shoes. I leave my hair down and do lots of mascara and a little gloss. My jeans, a white tee.

I gather everything I need from Ballard Market and pedal to Golden Gardens with grocery tote bags over each shoulder.

I take off my shoes and wait on a bench near the parking lot. The sand underneath my toes is a reminder that summer really is coming.

Nick shows up with a blanket, like I asked. We set out strawberries, sodas, and candy.

Holly shows up with Wilson, in his car. They hold hands as they walk over to us. She's as sunny as ever.

"Your hair," Holly says, mouth open.

"Funky, isn't it?" Nick says.

"I haven't seen it that color since sixth grade. It's going to take some getting used to."

"I'm already used to it," I say.

"I do like it." She holds up her hand, and Wilson's. "You guys know Wilson. Well, sort of."

He looks at us. He shakes Nick's hand, and he looks me in the eyes. "We know each other a little."

"Yeah," I say. "I'm glad we'll be getting to know each other better."

They sit down and we all open sodas. "Actually," Wilson says, "I've been meaning to thank you, Vanessa."

"Thank me?" The necklace. The note.

"I told him about it," Holly says.

"I get why Holly didn't love what you did at first, but I'm really, really glad she and I finally talked. We have so much in common." He grins. "And she's so gorgeous, I was afraid to talk to her!"

Holly turns pink. She's looking only at him when she says, "I'm glad we met too." But I know she's telling me something also. She's over it.

"Tell us about the dance," Nick says. "Full details."

Holly launches into a description of our school's gym all dressed up in twinkle lights, and tells us how the DJ was really bad but that made it fun. "I only wish you guys had been there," she says. Wilson puts his arm around her.

"Me too," Nick says. That zings me a little.

"We'll all do some fun stuff together this summer," I say. "When I'm not working with the kids and Holly's not practicing and Nick's not working on his comic and Wilson's not . . . What do you do, Wilson?"

"Violin, mostly. This summer, I'll be starting to prep for music scholarship auditions." He's really a great match for Holly. "We're working on a duet," he says.

"Like, Wilson's composing it." Holly looks so proudly at him. I grin at her.

"Well, there's something coming up that I hope you'll all want to go to," Nick says.

I think about it. "Fourth of July? Of course! We'll all go to the Gasworks fireworks together!"

Holly and Wilson nod.

"That'd be great," Nick says, "but I was thinking of the Pride Parade."

I think my heart skips two beats. He looks at me and continues. "It's a good idea. Will be fun to see what the parade's all about."

"Abso-snootly." And it will be fun. We'll just check it out. No expectations.

"We're in," Wilson says.

Holly adds, "Yep. I hear there are some really good marching bands."

"You are such a geek for music," I say. "That's what I like about you." I turn to Nick. "And you are the comic geek."

"You're one to talk," Nick says. "Art geek!"

"That's me."

I pass around the strawberries, and the afternoon is beautiful.

Acknowledgments

Vanessa was a hard girl to get to know (she does tend to keep up a bit of a tough exterior). Lots of people were very patient with me while I made this new friend, and I thank them.

Thanks to my parents, Eileen and Terry Gallagher, and my brother and SiL, Sean and Susan Gallagher.

To my writing friends, especially: Heather Davis, for the title help, the writing check-ins, and the fun distractions from this thing we both do. Kevin Emerson, for turning out to be more than just a guy in the coffee shop. Jackie Parker, for your valuable perspective as a voracious YA reader. Lara Zeises, for the cross-country friendship.

To the readergirlz community and the writers and readers of *Through the Tollbooth*.

To the librarians in Seattle, King County, and the surrounding areas. The booksellers, too. All of you are my people.

To the teens I've worked with and the readers I'm proud to share my stories with.

To Rosemary Stimola, my agent, who makes it possible for characters who exist in my mind to live on the bookshelves, too.

To Kate Gartner for a cover design that is so beautifully Vanessa.

To Wendy Lamb, Dana Carey, Caroline Meckler, and the rest of the team at Random House Children's Books for taking my words and thoughts and making them into a book. You are brilliant.